RAGING SWORDS
BOOK ONE OF THE DURLINDRATH SERIES

Robert Ryan

Cover Design by www.bookcoverartistry.com

ISBN-13 978-0-9942054-2-1
(print edition)

Trotting Fox Press

I0458104

Contents

1. Death or Infamy

Brand woke. His heart thrashed in his chest. His stomach churned, and the blood in his veins ran chill. But he spared no thought for any of those things.

He lay still, wrapped in his bedclothes, while his eyes strained to see and his ears to detect whatever had roused him from forgotten dreams.

It felt cold. It was dark also, being in that last stretch of night when the hours were long and the dawn, though near, was not yet come. It was that period when the human spirit ebbed lowest, where wills were weakest and shadows pooled the most deeply.

He saw nothing out of place. He heard no noise that should not have been. Yet his heart raced ever faster, and sweat, cold and clammy, trailed down his face and onto his throat like the lingering fingers of ghosts.

All through the city a questing breeze touched and pulled and tweaked at anything loose. A weather vane creaked as it turned on some high roof. A stable door banged unheeded, and in the palace where Brand lay shivering white curtains danced palely in the open windows.

He concentrated on the breeze. He did not like it. The open window near his bed looked over the city, but he saw nothing amiss far below. Yet the air was unnaturally cold on his face. Even as the thought came to him its fluttering movement stilled. The curtains ceased their billowing, and the cobbled streets below grew quiet once more.

He let out a long breath and relaxed. All he heard now was a whisper of air down the corridor outside his room and the faint creak of doors.

The warmth under the blankets began to soothe him back to sleep. The day was not yet begun. There was no need to stir. He could rest a little while longer and gather his strength for the toils yet to come.

Nor was he even wanted here, not among this foreign people. They did not like him. They did not respect him. They thought him far too young for his high position. Yet he had spilled his blood in deadly battles to serve them, defied death for their benefit, but most would still like to see his back, to see him walk off into the wild lands from whence he came.

And that was his desire – he ached to return to his homeland – to walk the paths that once he knew and to reclaim the life that had been stolen from him. Yet ties of loyalty held him, and he would not break them. The king of Cardoroth was a great man. To him he owed much, and he would serve and help in any way that he could.

Brand stirred, restless once more. Almost he had been lulled, but he knew sorcery when he felt it. Through a fog that dimmed his thoughts he forced himself to sit up in bed. His head suddenly cleared. Many in the city might wish him gone, but not the king. Gilhain trusted him. He had given him opportunity when others had not, and respect when others offered only disdain.

Gilhain! The last dregs of confusion scattered. Sorcery was afoot and the king would be its target. Brand leapt out of bed. No time he had to don chain mail or helm or the white surcoat of his station. He pulled on trousers and boots, drew the sword of his forefathers from its ancient sheath, and ran bare chested to the door.

He put his hand to the metal knob. The cold he felt there shocked him like a blow. He flung it open anyway and let go swiftly. Immediately a blast of frigid air assailed him, and as he ran the length of the corridor he saw frost on the marble floor and the iciness of it bit his unshod feet.

"Durlin!" he called loudly, summoning the king's bodyguards who slept in rooms along the passageway.

He sprinted ahead, but he saw nobody and heard no reply.

"Durlin!" he yelled again. "To the king!"

The door to Gilhain's chamber was now before him. The two Durlin stationed there lay slumped on the ground. A quick glance told him that they were dead, though no blood marked their white surcoats.

Beneath the door strange lights flickered, and he heard the first call of any person beside himself.

"Guards!" It was the queen. Fear gripped her voice and made it shrill.

A moment he hesitated, knowing that on the other side sorcery and mayhem filled the room and that he would likely die if he entered. But he was the Durlindrath, leader of the bodyguards, and when he swore his oath to protect the king he had done so from the heart.

He kicked with all his might. The door, built of sturdy oak slabs to protect against assault, did not budge. But the metal of the bolt that held it in place shattered within its icy casing. Shards from the ruined doorjamb flew into the air, and the door careened inward on its great hinges.

Brand sprang into the king's chamber. The rapid breath from his heaving chest turned to mist before him.

Yet more vapor, like a roiling fog, swirled within the room. There was no frost here, for the floor was laid with deep carpet, but ice hung in ribbons from the windows and sheeted the marble walls.

Gilhain and the queen were held at bay against the far wall. The king grasped a mighty sword in his two hands while she raised high a long knife. Six figures pressed toward them. They were wraithlike, gray and vaporous as the fog that eddied in the room. They glided on tall legs and their long arms reached forward like creeping fingers of mist toward the king's throat. The wraiths had faces: gaunt, cold-eyed and cruel. A pale light lit their hollow cheeks and glimmered silver-white in their trailing hair.

Brand had seen enough. He leaped toward them and yelled the battle cry of the Durlin: *Death or infamy!*

He attacked. His sword sliced and cut and stabbed. The wraiths were more solid than they looked, and he drew from them shuddering screams, yet their cries came as though from a great distance, and the creatures did not die. Instead of falling, three of the six turned upon him.

They reached for his throat, and one found a grip there. He felt the cold touch of death. But his sword was a Halathrin blade, forged by immortals, and though what would have been death-strokes to a man had not yet killed the wraiths, it certainly caused harm. He drove the blade forward into the closest figure until it staggered back, and then he jumped free from more reaching arms.

The creatures pressed their attack against him. And they barred the way to the king that he had sworn to protect. But they ignored the queen. And that was an error, for she fought with animal fury, and one of her deep thrusts slew a wraith whose misty form dispersed into the air with a shriek. The king, meanwhile, held the others off with deft strokes. But time was running out.

Brand swung and stabbed, holding the enemy off but not defeating them. Yet this much he had achieved: the enemy must now divide their attack that otherwise, concentrated on Gilhain alone, would by now have killed him.

He danced to the left and hewed at the outstretched arm of a foe. The blade did not sever it, but the follow up stroke drove deep into vaporish innards and Brand pushed the blade up and through to its hilt.

There was no heart to pierce, for these things drew no breath, and no blood surged through their bodies to enliven their limbs. Yet still, whatever sorcery gave them substance to kill by hand must needs also give them a physical form that might be damaged.

A moment the wraith was close to him. If it were a man they would have stood eye to eye. But in that haggard face he saw no gaze that mirrored his own. Instead, he perceived the flicker of lights and shadow coming to him as though through a fog, and he caught a sudden glimpse of a room, dark and shadow-laden, and he heard the dim sound of faraway chanting.

Before he understood whatever it was that he had heard and seen the wraith reeled back from him, but then, even as it began to sweep forward again in renewed attack, the sorcery that held it together faltered. It hissed and faded into formless vapor.

At last he heard running feet in the corridor. Light flashed from the doorway, dazzling bright. The gutted candles flared with leaping flame. The dark hearth burst with a fury of sparks and shimmering embers. Crackling flame roared to life.

Aranloth had come. He held his staff before him, and the diadem on his brow gleamed in the flaring light. The king's wizard now contended with the sorcery, and the room became furnace-hot. The sheeted ice dripped from the walls. The wraiths screeched and writhed, trying to evade the blades that now cut them with ease. Swift they

7

died, or else sharp steel sent them back to the pit dark sorcery had conjured them from.

In the sudden silence Brand heard from afar the enemy that had laid siege to Cardoroth. From beyond the city wall the chanting of an army rose to a crescendo, but then trailed off into a din of confusion and discord. Their war drums continued to beat, holding order longer, but soon even their thrumming voices stilled.

Brand heaved for breath. Was any place now safe for the king? A host of mankind's ancient enemies gathered without, trying to break in and destroy. Yet now sorcery had slipped even inside the palace. Nowhere seemed beyond the reach of the enemy who sought Gilhain's death. And well they might, for only his brilliance and tactics had forestalled them. Without him, Cardoroth would long since have fallen, and they knew it and hated him.

Brand looked at Gilhain. It was his job, his sworn oath, to keep the man safe. And neither blade nor shaft nor poison – neither a thousand foes nor a lone assassin, not even sorcery in the night would avail against him, so long as he drew breath.

But the dead guards in the corridor reminded him that a man, no matter the strength of his will, regardless of his love and loyalty, might still be outmatched.

It was nearly so tonight. The reach of the enemy was somehow longer than it had been, and the hope of the city dwindled further. For the enemy *did* outmatch them.

The elug host was vast. The siege of Cardoroth could not be broken, and the enemy would likely prevail. If not tonight, then in a month, or six months. All the swifter if the king died, and that the enemy knew and strove to achieve – any way it could.

Brand sensed that the doom of Cardoroth was coming. By what means the enemy grew stronger rather than weaker, he could not guess. Sorcery had never yet struck so deep into the city. Always Aranloth and his like prevented it. Yet not tonight. Perhaps never again.

He saw the same understanding when he looked into Gilhain's eyes. But there was determination there also, an unflinching will, and Brand admired it.

The king might die, but if so, he would not be alone at the end.

2. Too Many Enemies

Brand had many questions for Aranloth, but his first task was the king's welfare. And the queen's, for to her he also owed much.

He strode toward the bed where they now sat together, and the sight of them holding hands and shivering from the effect of cold, or shock, having just survived a sorcerous attempt on their lives wrenched his heart. They deserved better than this. Yet assassination attempts were not uncommon. This was not the first, nor would it be the last. That the previous Durlindrath, and every Durlin who served him, was dead offered proof enough of that.

Brand pulled up a heavy blanket and draped it over them.

"Thank you," Gilhain said. The man still gripped his sword so tightly in one hand that his knuckles were white.

The queen did not speak. But she looked at him. It was a gaze that said much, for he was close to her counsels and understood better than most the mixed pride, love and fear that underpinned her marriage to the king. Her look told him that this was perhaps the closest attempt yet on the life of the man that she loved.

Brand knew that she was made of steel, a fit partner for a great king, but he knew also that even steel could break, and he saw the shattering recognition in her eyes that this could not go on. Sooner or later an attempt would succeed. But he knew also, both from past conversations and the glint in her eye now, that she would never give in to despair. She had her husband's back, and Brand wished there was a girl like that in his own life.

At that moment soldiers and servants bustled into the room. It grew suddenly loud, and Brand walked away to leave them to their ministrations. He wanted a chance to think.

He moved to the hearth. The naked blade in his hand now felt out of place, but he did not put it down. He stood close to the fire and felt the first touches of warmth return to his skin. He fed more wood to the flames, enjoying both the heat and the smell of smoke. It brought back memories of childhood campfires in a land far from here.

Aranloth joined him. The old man leaned on his staff. He seemed ordinary again, shrunken back to humanity, but it was only a veil for the power that he possessed. For he was as strong and swift as any young warrior, though old as the hills and possessed of lore and magic that could not be gathered save over the span of many lifetimes.

"That marks the third attempt this month," the old man said.

Brand stared into the leaping flames. "Yet the first of sorcery."

"Yes, and that makes me wonder. The enemy does not possess the strength to break through the wards that I and my kind use to protect the city. The walls and gate are always at risk, for we cannot be everywhere, and they are the focus of the attack. But here, in the heart of Cardoroth, we deemed it safe."

Brand looked at him for the first time. "Perhaps other sorcerers have joined the army?"

"I don't think so. There are thirteen, which is a number they favor, and I do not believe they have added to it."

"Then how have they broken through?" Brand immediately regretted that his words sounded like an accusation.

"I wish I knew. It's your part to protect against blade, arrow and poison. Mine against sorcery. Neither of us have failed – until tonight. I don't know how they got passed me, but I'll discover it, one way or another."

"I didn't mean to suggest that it was your fault. You've done more than anybody to keep the king alive."

"But it wasn't enough tonight. If not for you, then I would have been too late."

Brand ran a hand through his hair. "How did they do it? What *were* those wraiths?"

"They were drùghoth; sendings your people would call them. Something has changed. The sorcerers don't have the strength for that. Not these ones anyway, and not over that distance. It's several miles between where they lay siege to the wall and where we stand here."

Brand let out a sigh. "As you say, something has changed. But if there aren't more sorcerers, then what can it be?"

Aranloth stared bleakly into the fire. "I don't know. But if I don't discover the reason for their increased strength…" he paused, "or the artifact that they're now using, then I cannot prevent further attacks. They'll certainly try again. They nearly succeeded this time."

Brand turned, for the king had left the servants to tend his wife. He no longer looked like a man who had just faced death. There was nothing to be read in his eyes; they held the same sharp intelligence, the same wolfish stare as always. Perhaps he was used to it by now.

"Once more you've saved me," he said to Brand. "And my wife this time as well. What reward can I give you?"

Brand shrugged. "To serve is reward enough, My King. To defy your enemy, who is also the enemy of my people, is … satisfying also."

"Come! There must be something?" Gilhain pressed.

Brand shook his head. "The one thing that I wish above all else, my family and my rightful place among my own people, is something beyond even the power of a king of Cardoroth."

The king looked at him sadly. The wolfish gaze turned to pity.

"Those things I would give, and gladly, if I could, though it meant that Cardoroth lost its bravest man, and I a friend. But if I cannot give you that, then take at least my thanks, and those of the queen. They're heartfelt."

Brand bowed. They were high compliments, and he found no words in answer.

Gilhain turned to Aranloth. "Come, old friend. We must speak. This latest turn bodes ill for the realm, and we have much to discuss."

Brand left them to it. He had other duties now. He walked to the doorway where the bodies of the two Durlin lay.

The others of his order had gathered there. Their faces were grim, and they did not speak. Of the thirty, the *new* thirty that he had himself handpicked since the previous Durlindrath and his men were killed, there were now only twenty-eight. He did not doubt that soon there would be less. And it was hard to find good men these days. Guarding the king was a job that few were suited to, and fewer still were willing to suffer its risks.

He looked down at the dead men, and the creed of the Durlin ran through his thoughts:

Tum del conar — El dar tum!
Death or infamy — I choose death!

These men had been given no choice. They were slain by sorcery in the night. Yet they had still chosen to serve the king, to protect and guard him, to swear their oaths of loyalty. In their way, they *did* choose death, for they knew when they joined the Durlin that Gilhain would be attacked, if not how.

Brand gazed at them somberly. How long before someone looked down at his own dead body the same way, tallying up the long record of those who had died before him?

There were too many enemies, both outside of Cardoroth and inside. For there were traitors within the walls also. Less powerful than the sorcerers, but cunning, determined and cloaked in secrecy. Yet there was honor to set against it. The Durlin were legendary, and often the mere sight of their white surcoats in the city streets brought cheers from the crowd.

Soldiers arrived with stretchers, and Brand made a sign for his men to take them. They gently moved the bodies across. Brand lifted up the end of one by its wooden handles, bearing the weight of a dead man that he felt responsible for.

He made a signal to four of the Durlin. "Stay here," he said. "Keep a close eye on things, for there are now many coming to see the king, and that could be taken as an opportunity. Let no one in who does not need to be here."

"Yes, Durlindrath," they answered.

Slowly the stretcher-bearers moved down the corridor, and the remaining Durlin followed. One led them, holding a single candle in his hand, and as they went the men chanted softly the words that had come down through the long years for such a procession. It was grim, but sonorous in their deep voices, and it held a certain grace.

Wherever they met palace staff in the corridors the men and women stood still and bowed their heads in respect. Some cried quietly, perhaps those new to the palace who had not seen this as often as others who had served longer.

Down they went until at length they reached the chapterhouse of the Durlin on the ground floor. They walked through the great doorway, crafted of carved oak posts and into the ancient rooms set aside for their use since the building of the palace some eight hundred years ago.

The walls were paneled with oak, broken by massive arched doorways that led to an outer courtyard. But many old hangings decorated the walls, woven in their threads the story of the Durlin since their founding and the many brave deeds that they had done.

The vaulted roof was high above, and the chanting of the men grew deeper while the ceiling threw down their voices again in matching echoes of mourning.

Brand felt the weight of the dead man that he carried. Somewhere his story would be added to one of the newer hangings.

His footsteps slowed as they came to a central dais. Here the men would be laid in state until their funeral. Carefully, they moved the bodies across onto the cold stone, the same red granite from which much of the city was built, only this was polished and carved with symbols.

The chanting of the men ceased. They stood now in a circle around the dais, joining hand to hand and standing with bowed heads. It was now silent.

Brand closed his eyes. A minute they would stand like this, showing their respect, and then their duties would call again to serve the king.

He could not help but wonder that it was a small amount of time; but not hours nor weeks would bring them back. There was no weeping as there would have been in his homeland. The people of Cardoroth were stern and proud, though death touched them just as deeply. And if they stood now in a grand building, instead of in a thatched hut; if they were silent instead of weeping, it did not change anything. There was love and respect in the room, and that was all that mattered. And that was the same whether here or at home.

But thinking of home drew memories to his mind. He wanted to walk there again, beneath its trees and sun, to once more climb its green hills and look out over its wide lands, to cross its rivers and hear the sound of the cattle lowing on the wind. But he could not. His loyalty belonged to the king. Now more than ever.

The silence was over, and the group became restless.

"Durlin," he said. "These two men have paid a high price. They gave freely of what they had so little – time. For there is always much that we dream of, and in the end much that is left undone before age, sickness or death robs us of our abilities."

The men looked at him. Their expressions showed little, but they heard his words and understood them. He was one of them, and there were certain truths that they all knew, even if they rarely spoke them. And they knew what he would say next, because they had heard him say it before.

"Yet these men chose freely, as do we all, to guard the king. But it is not so much the king that they died to protect, but the ideal of what is good in the world. Today, they served justice. Today, they struck a blow for the people against the forces of chaos. Today, alone and in the dark, they gave of their lives so that there may yet be other days where truth and justice and honor and goodwill shine in the world." He paused, looking at the dead men. "We will not forget them."

The men gave the ritual reply: "Long will we remember them."

At his sign two Durlin retrieved a flag from a redwood cabinet nearby and draped it over the bodies. It was made of the same thick cloth as their surcoats, gleaming and shining, but whereas they wore no sign or emblem on their clothes the flag was woven with their insignia: seven red stars that represented the seven sons of the first king of Cardoroth, all of whom formed his guard. Three had died to protect him, and these were woven on the top. Beneath them were the other four. Separating them was the Durlin creed, uttered by the first son to die while he defended his father from attack:

Tum del conar – El dar tum!
Death or infamy – I choose death!

Brand took a last look. There was nothing else he could do for these men. Now, he must turn his thoughts to the king and how best to protect him from attack. He could not rely on Aranloth to stymy the sorcery. The enemy had somehow gained an advantage, and courage might now be asked to achieve what wizardry could not.

His second and third in command understood what he was thinking and approached. They knew him well, from even before his time as Durlindrath, and they guessed he would have instructions.

He nodded to them. "Lornach. Taingern – let's go to the courtyard. I'll feel better if I can breathe some fresh air, away from death and sorcery."

They followed him through one of the great arches and into the gray half-light just before dawn. The courtyard was paved with smooth flagstones, though at its further end it was grassed.

This was where the Durlin trained. A mass of weapons and armor hung from every wall. These were the tools of their trade, and Brand knew them better than most men living – else he would be dead. But he would rather hold a horse's reins than a halberd's handle. He preferred the tilling of the earth and the sweet smell of newly opened ground where things would grow instead of the hacking and cutting and bludgeoning that brought death. But few men chose their destiny. It chose them.

"What now?" Lornach asked.

Brand turned to one of his few friends in the city, and one of his oldest. He knew him better as Shorty, but that was unbecoming for the high station of a Durlin.

"The king should not be alive," he said. The two men looked at him strangely, and he gave them a faint smile. "What I mean is that our chances of keeping him alive have always been slim. And that has been the case for a long time. We fight a losing battle, one we should have lost long ago, and from now on it will only get worse."

"You paint a picture of little hope," Taingern said.

"There is no hope," he replied. "We three know it. And so do the rest of the Durlin. But they do not have our experience. They do not know that fate favors the bold-hearted, as we have learned ourselves. For we also, just as the king, should be dead."

"That may be so," Lornach said. "But how does it help them?"

"We survived our past perils, and there were certainly enough of them, by believing in ourselves. We did not despair. And a way of survival opened up. Of course, we were lucky too, but a person makes their own luck. So this much we must do for them. We know they are prepared to die to try to save the king. And likely all of us will, but we cannot allow them to resign themselves to that fate, or it will come all the swifter. We must remind them at every opportunity that there is hope, even if it cannot be seen, and to fight to the last, with not only courage but also cunning. That way at least some of them may survive."

The three men looked at each other grimly. Their task was not now only to keep the king alive, but the Durlin also. It would be the hardest job of their lives, and they knew it.

They walked back inside. The Durlin had returned to their duties. The room was empty except for the two corpses. Soon men would come to prepare them for their long rest. There would be a funeral, full of pomp and ceremony. They would be praised with great praise. But nothing would bring them back. Not the gray-eyed Gernlik who could never keep his white surcoat clean, nor the red-haired Carangar, always quiet and somber, but merry as a country maid when he drank too much.

The three men went their separate ways. Taingern was in charge until mid-morning, and for a little while Brand had a chance to get some rest.

He returned to his chamber and slipped back under the covers, but he did not put aside his sword. He feared to do so, for he did not know when, or in what manner, the next attack would come. He gripped the hilt even in his sleep, and through a fog of slumber and half-waking he heard the war drums of the enemy begin to beat, the enemy that had haunted other cities, other realms and other times before this. The enemy that had harried mankind for long ages of the land of Alithoras: elugs.

The beating drums rose to a faster pace, and then the chanting of the enemy soldiers began. It too had been heard outside the walls of many besieged cities before this. Some still stood. Many did not. Brand tossed and turned as the fell words floated through the heavy air:

Ashrak ghùl skar! Skee ghùl ashrak!
Skee ghùl ashrak! Ashrak ghùl skar!

The chant flowed without beginning or end. The drums hastened. Stamping boots thundered, and dread wove itself through the shadow-world of Brand's half sleep. He heard the hateful words, and understood them:

Death and destruction! Blood and death!
Blood and death! Death and destruction!

The dark words ran through the streets and drowned out birdsong and the crowing of roosters as the dawn shone golden on the high domes and lofty roofs of the city.

In his sleep Brand heard knocking at his door. Or was it elug war drums in the palace? He leapt out of bed, sword in hand, his chest heaving for air.

But it was no attack. Aranloth stood in the doorway, the white robes of his office lit by morning sun shining through the window and the oaken staff in his hand gleaming gold. If he was alarmed by the sword levelled at him or the sudden reaction, he gave no sign of it.

"Come with me," he said. "I have an errand on the city walls, and I would like you to be there with me."

Brand picked up his scabbard from a nearby table and sheathed his blade.

"I dare not leave the palace. The king is in too much danger."

Aranloth leaned on the staff. "So he is. He's always in danger. But he'll survive an hour or two without you. I need you now more than he does, and Gilhain has given his leave. He knows whence I go and what I seek."

Brand let out a long breath and some of his tension went with it. He was still wearing his trousers and boots, so all he needed to do was put on a shirt and his white surcoat, and then belt on his sword.

When he was ready they went to the palace stables and retrieved their mounts. Brand rode his black stallion, a massive horse, but one that still mustered great speed at need and that could endure long hours of toil at a slower pace. Aranloth rode a young roan gelding.

They trotted down the streets, and the people looked at them as they went. Both were well known, and their clothes showed who they were well before their faces came into view.

Aranloth took the road to Arach Neben, the West Gate. It was chiefly there that the enemy had established its camp. They did not surround the whole city. Rather, they concentrated their force on one length of wall.

It was a long ride. Aranloth did not speak much during it, for he was deep in thought, and Brand did not disturb him. What he pondered was obviously troubling, and Brand was not eager to learn it, though he guessed that he would, whether he wanted to or not, when they reached their destination.

They stabled their mounts at the bottom of one of the guard towers that flanked the gate. Then, ascending many stairs, they came at length to the top of the tower.

Brand knew it well. In this very place he had served for some time, and the view of the walls to either side and the open lands stretching out to the west he knew well. But it all looked different now.

Below was the enemy camp. It spread out, sprawling and vast. It threw out wings to encircle the city, but these were no more than picket lines to prevent Cardoroth's scouts from entering or leaving.

The main host remained on the west side and concentrated their attack on that wall. For a month they had done so, but the city had food and water to last for years. It was a stalemate, as all sieges were, and yet by force of numbers and a persistence of effort over a long time the enemy might break through. The constant battle against fear, and the sorcerous chanting of the enemy during the night where their power was exerted to weaken the morale of the defenders, took a slow but inevitable toll.

Brand and Aranloth looked at the enemy camp. The sorcerers were in a tent in the midst of the host. They were surrounded by rank after rank of elugs, fell creatures with gray-green tinged skin, malicious eyes and harsh voices. They were a cruel people, apt subjects of the sorcerers, and they fought with an ancient enmity for mankind, born out of a time of legend, for battles had been fought with them since before the Camar races of men came east and founded realms along the coastal lands of Alithoras. And the Duthenor, Brand's own people, fought with them in ancient times also, although his ancestors migrated eastward much later and in fewer numbers than the great waves of Camar tribes.

All along the battlement wall, which the people often called the Cardurleth, the king's soldiers held their stations. They relaxed while they could for no assault was being made at present. But men skilled with blade and shaft were not the only ones who defended the wall. Spread thinly among them were white-robed and staff-carrying wizards.

Aranloth spoke briefly with the captain of the tower and he led his men away, filing down the stairs to leave the two of them alone.

"What if the enemy attacks?" Brand asked.

"The men won't be far away. They have only gone down one level and can return swiftly. But the enemy is not going to attack for a while."

Brand was alone with the wizard, and he sensed that something would soon happen, something of importance.

"So, what's our purpose here?" he asked.

Aranloth looked at him grimly. His face was unreadable, as it usually was, but there was a look to his eyes that spoke of some emotion beneath the surface, though what it was Brand could not tell.

"I'm going to attempt something …" he said.

Brand studied him more closely. He saw no fear, but there was worry, and that concerned him. For whatever Aranloth was going to do, it must be dangerous, perhaps exceedingly so, and the wizard did not take such risks without great need.

3. Use the Sword!

Aranloth looked over the battlement at the enemy.

"Out there is the host, and it's monstrous in size and temperament, but its head is the small group of sorcerers – elùgroths to give them their proper name. They are the beating heart of the enemy, and its mind also. Not only that, they are the source of the drùghoth, the sendings that last night nearly killed the king. If I would learn whence came the power to achieve that, if I would learn more of the elùgroths' intentions, then I must seek that knowledge from them."

"And how will you do that?"

"By the only means that I can. I'm a lòhren, the oldest of the wizards, and there are skills that we lòhren have, even if we use them but rarely. One I will employ now."

Brand thought about that. "It seems obvious that the skill of which you speak is only used rarely for a reason. I assume it's dangerous?"

"Yes. It's dangerous. Lethal if done incorrectly, and even then there are perils that…" he paused, considering his words. "Let's just say that it's dangerous. But it's also necessary, and I'll risk it. For that purpose I have brought you along."

"How can I help? I'm willing to do anything you ask, but I haven't got any affinity for magic."

Aranloth gave an unexpectedly broad grin. "You're quick to agree to help given that you don't know what I'll do. That's dangerous with a lòhren, but in this case you need not fear. Only I'll be at risk."

"What exactly will you do?"

"I'll free my spirit from the shackles of the flesh and enter the otherworld, the world that hangs between life and death. There, with spirit eyes I'll enter the camp, enter the very tent of the elùgroths and discern what it is they do. And how."

Brand raised an eyebrow. "No wonder it's dangerous."

"It is what it is," Aranloth said. "But with your aid I can lessen the danger. The chief risk is that I won't be able to return to my body. If that happens, I'll wither and die. That will be your task – to call me back should I fail to do so on my own."

"And how will I know that you're in such straights?"

"I'll talk to you as I go and tell you what's happening. You'll know what I know, and should I fail to speak for any length of time you must wake me straight away. Use your sword and prick my flesh, even to the point of drawing blood. That strengthens the tie between spirit and body, and should pull me back."

Brand noticed that Aranloth said *should* rather than *will*, but he let it go. Now was not the time to show any doubt.

"I'll get you back, so long as you don't hold it against me that I strike you with a sword. The blade of my forefathers is sharp, and I'm unused to being gentle with it."

"Don't worry. You won't hurt me badly. But just remember, I'm not an elug. You need do no more than draw blood. If that doesn't work, nothing will."

"Let's get started then," Brand said. "The sooner this is over the better I'll like it. Magic always makes me uneasy."

"That's as it should be," Aranloth said. "It's what separates lòhrens from elùgroths. My kind use power sparingly, for its use is two-sided; the power affects us as

25

much as we it. Too much is dangerous, yet the elùgroths don't forgo it, and especially they force their wills on others to try to dominate them, and the sorcery changes them according to how they use it. But enough! I'm talking now merely to put this off. We'll begin at once."

Aranloth sat down cross-legged on the stone. He let his staff rest in his lap, and he held it with his left hand while his right sought Brand's and took it in the warrior's grip, wrist to wrist.

"Do not let go," he said. "This helps me anchor into the world of the living."

Brand gripped his hand firmly. He would not let go. But he held his Halathrin blade in his right, drawn free from the sheath and ready to use if the lòhren needed recalling.

For long moments nothing happened. Aranloth's breathing was deep and long, but it grew ever slower, and he used his belly rather than his chest. His eyes were closed, the lids barely fluttering, and the clear skin on his face remained rosy with health. He showed no real signs of his age. But the grip of his hand lessened a little in intensity, and his head began to lean ever so slightly to one side.

Brand was startled when Aranloth sighed. It was like the last breath of a dying man, but the lòhren spoke to him a moment later.

"I am free," he said. "Here it is dark, but I still see the camp before us. I float down to the enemy as a leaf on the airs, though no leaf is this light. All about are shadows, and the elugs flit through them, groping forms of malice, but afar, in their midst, is a deeper shadow that not even my spirit eyes can pierce."

Brand felt his heart race and slowed his breathing to calm down. The lòhren's hand was now cold to touch, and as the words came to him of the camp and the

26

shadows they formed a vivid picture in his mind as though they were part of a waking dream. Aranloth had not warned of that, and he was troubled, for it seemed to him that this was not quite what the lòhren expected.

"I slip among them," Aranloth continued. "The elugs do not see me, but I feel their hate, and their fear, and most of all I sense their uncertainty. That is why they do not attack this morning. They are leaderless for the moment. The elùgroths give no commands, and it seems that they were hurt last night when the Drùghoth were dispatched. They recover from their efforts."

There was a pause. Aranloth did not speak, yet Brand had the impression of sweeping movement and dark shapes lurching beneath him like a stream of water where fish swam but all that was glimpsed was the flash of tails, fins and the momentary turn and glide of bodies.

"I come now to the tent," Aranloth said.

Brand saw it. Vague – a thing of shadows deeper than all other shadows. It was guarded by power, warded with sorcery that he did not understand but still sensed.

"There is sorcery here," Aranloth said. It was needless, for Brand already knew it. That made him all the more uneasy.

The feeling of flight ceased. The tent was before them. A great construction of canvas, held in place by ropes and ties and wooden stakes.

It grew cold. The sun was so dim that it was but a shadowy patch in the sky less gray than elsewhere. Of the grass, there was no sign of green. Nor could Brand feel air on his face. But he felt the cold, both in Aranloth's handgrip and here near the elùgroths' tent.

"I go slowly now," Aranloth said.

The canvas came close. And then Brand was in it. He saw nothing for a moment but then once more on the other side dim images came to him.

There was but one room in the tent. It was bare of furniture and adornments. The ceiling was lost in shadows above. Yet at its center were deeper shadows, though he could distinguish nothing.

"They are here," Aranloth said, and his thought was a drift of nothingness on a silent breeze. "I must be careful or they'll sense me. Their wards are weak and ill crafted. My passing through did not give alarm, yet the closer I go the greater will be the risk."

The darkness seemed to gather and rush closer for a moment, and then it eased. The shadows were deep, but there was some little light from iron incense holders that smoldered a sullen red. A strange scent was in the air, sharp and repugnant. And it was clouded still further by drifting smoke from the slow burning of whatever bark-like material was in the holders.

Yet Brand could still see. Cushions and rugs covered the floor, and in a circle were the thirteen elùgroths. Most reclined as though resting. Some sat cross-legged as did Aranloth back at the top of the tower. A few muttered dully in some language beyond Brand's experience.

As though from a great distance Aranloth's voice drifted to him.

"They rest," he said. "And well they might, for the power they expended last night was great, and the destruction of the Drùghoth will have hurt them, for he who makes a thing must suffer some measure of harm when it is injured."

Brand remembered the hisses of pain from last night, and he smiled grimly. It gave him satisfaction that these sorcerers did not escape the assassination attempt unscathed.

"It's well for us that they're weary," Aranloth continued, "else they might more easily discover me."

They drifted a little closer, and Brand saw the enemy close up. They were black cloaked and hooded. Their dark wych-wood staffs rested in, or near, their pallid hands. Their skin, where he could see it, was white and blue-veined, as of a man who never saw the light of day. Of their faces, he could not see anything.

One there was who sat still and unmoving. He muttered the loudest, and at him Aranloth fixed his attention.

"Khamdar," he said. "A powerful elùgroth. Even for them he is a dark one. No evil is beyond him. Death and destruction trail in his wake, for he seeks admittance into the highest rank of their order. There is blood on his hands that all the oceans in the world would not wash away."

Aranloth paused, perhaps lost in memories of battles and destruction from other times and places. So Brand guessed. But he knew this: the lòhren's unease increased before he spoke again.

"Here we come to it at last. There is an object before them."

Brand looked closely. He could see nothing at first, but then they eased a little closer. Before them all, but most closely to Khamdar, he saw something.

It was long and dark. It rested on a thick black cloth, as though it was an object of reverence. There were marks on it, strange signs that either glowed and pulsed with a faint light of their own or else reflected dimly the smoldering embers in the incense holders.

"I am closer now," Aranloth said. "It is precious to them. It rests on velvet and is woven with marks of sorcery. It is … it is a wych-wood staff such as elùgroths use. Flexible as a whip, yet still strong enough to contain and conduct great power."

There was a longer pause, and Brand felt tension sing in the air as Aranloth's gaze swept over the elùgroths.

"Yet the thirteen each keep their staffs beside them."

There was another pause, and Aranloth drew closer still to the staff that lay on the black cloth.

"The staff is not whole. I see splinters and a shattered end. It is broken near the middle. The splinters are dagger-like and malice drips from them, cruel and potent, like venom from a poisoned blade."

The room seemed to grow colder. Or else a breeze touched their bodies far away atop the tower. Brand could not tell.

"I must get closer," Aranloth said. "This is a thing of power, and it fills me with dread. Arcane forces roil within it, trapped for many long years. They are become one with the wood, perhaps were infused into it for a purpose, designed to be one with it. It is far more than a staff … it is a repository of elùgai, the sorcery of an elùgroth. It fills it even as a carafe is filled with red wine. It is strange sorcery … one that perhaps I have felt before. I hope that is not so … but I must touch it to be sure."

In the shadows Brand saw Aranloth's hand glimmer palely. It reached out, wavering and silvery, barely there and yet visible to him.

The hand stretched forth, and then paused a moment before it finally rested against the dark wood.

Aranloth cried out in sudden pain. He tried to withdraw, but his hand seemed stuck. Some power within the staff gripped him.

The elùgroths stirred. Some that were lying came to their feet. Khamdar remained seated, but his eyes flicked open, dark slits of evil. His muttering grew suddenly clear in a chant of great force.

30

"The sword!" yelled Aranloth. "The sword! I'm trapped and cannot return!"

Brand felt the hilt of the blade in his hand. He grew suddenly dizzy, swaying between two places at once, for the scene in the dark tent was before his eyes, but so also was the bright light at the top of the tower and the seated lòhren.

He fumbled, bringing his sword to bear, and he ran the edge hard along Aranloth's arm where he took his own in the warrior's grip.

The Halathrin-forged steel drew blood. It ran, bright red, dripping onto the stone floor. Or was it the dark cloth beneath the broken staff? Brand could not be sure.

Aranloth groaned. His hand gripped tightly. His strength was much more than that of any old man, and Brand felt pain in his arm. But the lòhren did not return to his body, and the grip of his hand lessened. Nor did he speak again.

Brand concentrated on the dark scene in the tent once more, and the light of the sun vanished. Khamdar's chanting was grown shrill, as though he fought some battle against another power. More elùgroths joined him, assuming their positions in the circle, hands on their staffs.

"Aranloth!" Brand yelled. But there was no answer. He sensed the lòhren's presence, but he was caught amid some struggle for life and death, and Brand knew he was losing. The elùgroths held his spirit in the tent by the power they possessed and by the force of the broken staff. He would die here unless something happened.

Brand looked around. The dark tent swam. The chill in the air grew, and frost formed on the stems of the metal incense holders. He felt sorcery, strong and dark, sure of purpose and growing. Suddenly, Brand saw the woven threads of it through the room, like a spider's web, drawing tighter, growing thicker, and he knew that if he did not do something soon then not only would Aranloth be caught in this trap, but he himself would also be held by it, and they would both die.

4. The Long Hidden

Brand hesitated.

He should return to his body while he still could. But it was not in his nature to leave Aranloth behind, and he knew if he did that he would regret it. And things would go ill for the city and the king, as if they had not done so enough.

He gripped hard the hilt of his Halathrin blade and made his choice: *fate favored the bold-hearted!* With a wild yell and a mighty swing he brought the sword crashing against Khamdar's head.

The elùgroth recoiled, sprawling away, and then he rose towering to his feet, the tallest man Brand had ever seen. His head swung from side to side, his smoldering eyes, lit red like the embers in the incense holders, roved the tent seeking his assailant. On his head there was no wound, yet pain showed on his face. And surprise.

Brand had not expected to hurt him, had not even been sure that the elùgroth would feel anything, and yet he had achieved his aim. Khamdar ceased to chant. The others seemed confused by his strange movements, and their own voices faltered.

It was the chance that Aranloth needed, for a moment it was the staff alone that held him, and with a surge of effort he broke free of its power. There was a rush of air and light. And then, as if from a great distance, the voice of Khamdar followed. *You are dead, Aranloth. The city will fall about you and whoever it is that just helped you. I will know them if we meet. He shall not escape me either!*

Light flashed around Brand and dazzled his eyes, bringing tears to them. Yet he could see, and he knew he was on the top of the tower again. The morning was about them, and the enemy left behind below.

He turned his gaze to Aranloth. The lòhren struggled to his feet, using his staff to help him, and Brand rose also.

They looked at each other, and the lòhren shook his head as if to clear it.

"That was close," he said. "Closer and more risky than I guessed. They knew I might try such a thing, and that did not worry me, but I was not prepared for the staff. It is a thing of greater power than I expected, and that misjudgment nearly undid me."

Brand used an old cloth to wipe the drops of Aranloth's blood from his blade and then sheathed the sword.

"All is well as ends well," he said. "At least it's so in this case. We came back, and you must have learned what you needed to know about their new powers. It seemed to me that you recognized the staff."

Aranloth raised an eyebrow. "We'll get to that in a moment. Don't you know what happened in there?"

"It was all a bit vague," Brand answered with a frown. "But you were caught, both by the staff and the elùgroths working some sorcery."

"And then?"

"And then I struck Khamdar with my sword. It didn't seem to hurt him much, but it surprised him and gave you a chance to escape when his concentration faltered."

Aranloth stared at him. "And nothing about that struck you as strange?"

"I'm not sure what you mean. It was *all* strange."

Aranloth let out a long sigh. "I said when we began that I would describe things to you. But there was no need for that, was there? You were with me, as you should not have been. For someone who mistrusts magic you have a strange affinity for it."

Brand shrugged. "I *do* mistrust magic, and I want nothing to do with it. But I was there with you, and I saw what needed to be done, and I did it. Is there really anything strange about that?"

Aranloth looked like he would argue, but all he said was "Perhaps not." Then he leaned on his staff and looked out over the battlement.

"So," Brand said. "Tell me more of the staff. Where's it from, and what can you do about the power they take from it?"

The lòhren's gaze did not stray from the field below, but his eyes seemed to look back in time rather than at the enemy camp.

"It's a thing of power, that much you already know. But it has a history – one that is dark, both by the deeds done and by the long years that have piled uncounted since that time. The land of Alithoras has seen kingdoms rise from nothing and fall back into oblivion since last I saw it, and he that wielded it."

The lòhren paused and turned his keen-eyed glance upon Brand. There was anger in his eyes, but it was only the most obvious of the many emotions that swirled there, visible now as they rarely were, for the lòhren was mostly impassive. Something must have disturbed him greatly.

"The staff," he continued, "belonged to Shurilgar the Sorcerer. Shurilgar the Betrayer of Nations. Shurilgar, that once was a lòhren. It is a name not unknown to you, nor to any who dwell in Alithoras, though he lived in a past so long ago that most else is forgotten about it."

Brand knew the name. He knew it well, better than many. Shurilgar was one of the great ones, mighty among lòhrens … and among elùgroths. He knew him, and he feared him, though the sorcerer was dead.

The legends said that he was slain by Aranloth in a great battle. The lòhren did not talk of such things. If it was true, Brand did not know. It was hard to believe that the man who stood before him now, talking and breathing, was the same legendary Aranloth from those far distant times. And yet that was what was thought in Cardoroth, though some claimed the name of Aranloth was used by generations of lòhrens as a kind of hereditary title. Brand was not inclined to believe them. But none of this, intriguing as it was, helped solve Cardoroth's present problems.

"If they have this thing of power, why haven't they used it before?"

"They did not have it before. Of that we can be certain. If they had, they would have used it. Elùgroths are always quick to exploit such things, eager to unleash sorcery, quick to dismiss the consequences, and slow to exercise caution. But every consequence is one day discerned, every secret one day discovered. In this case, the long hidden is found again. The long sought for is now in their possession. And they *have* sought this thing, since before Cardoroth was founded. Before the Camar tribes came east and founded their realms, some of which still stand."

The lòhren turned to him once more. As always, he veiled the power that was in him, but Brand sensed it near the surface now, like the sun covered by the last trailing edges of a cloud, ready to blaze.

"It was I that defeated Shurilgar, as you have guessed. It was I that broke his power and slew him, though he was as a brother to me in a time more distant than that deed now is to you. And in doing so, I broke his staff. One half the immortal Halathrin took to their realm, for they were with me and suffered more than most from his betrayal and malice. There long ages they held it secure. The other half I kept myself."

"Why wasn't it destroyed?" Brand asked.

"Alas! I wish that it was. Such was my counsel, but it went unheeded, though you will see why. For the wood came from a sacred grove of elms in the forest realm of the Halathrin. Not only that, it grew on a mound, the burial place of their great king who led them hither to Alithoras on their exodus. It was from that place that Shurilgar stole the timber for his staff. For the Halathrin do not entomb their dead in stone, even their great ones. Yet this much they knew of their own lore, and needed not my telling: the staff was possessed of an evil power, yet they deemed that its power must lie dormant without an elùgroth to wield it. There, in their forest realm, they kept their half, and they kept it in token of the living tree and the rest of the grove that Shurilgar had razed by fire and sorcery. They would not destroy the staff, for it was all that was left of something sacred to them, even though it was now tainted. I did not agree with them then, still less do I do so now, and yet I understand why they took that path."

Aranloth had grown sad in the telling of this tale. Brand guessed that he understood better than most why people clung to the last remnant of something, or someone, that was loved after they were gone. In his long life he must have suffered many such losses.

The lòhren seemed to stiffen now with some resolve or new thought.

"But some dreadful deeds must have been done to retrieve it," he said, "and I fear for the Halathrin. Not lightly did they undertake to preserve and guard this thing, for they knew it would be sought by elùgroths. And to enter the Halathrin realm by force or stealth is unheard of. They have powers of their own, not that of lòhrens and elùgroths, but a unique and peculiar magic. And when that fails they have many bright blades and great courage. Alas, all of these things must have been tested and found wanting. They will feel shame that evil has been loosed on the land, and they will feel grief that all that is left of their sacred trust is stolen again."

Brand did not really grasp half of this story. But loss he understood. And evil. It was before him now anytime he chose to look over the battlement and watch the seething mass of the dark army spread below. But something else troubled him.

"What of the staff's second half? Was it destroyed? If not, how can you know which half the elùgroths found?"

Aranloth shook his head. "The second half was not destroyed. The two halves are joined by sorcery. To destroy one is to destroy the other, for they are linked by the forces that infuse them. And I had not the heart do that to the Halathrin."

"Then where is it?"

Aranloth looked at him bleakly. "It's in the one place in Alithoras that none can go save me. There only did I trust to its safekeeping, the only secure place for such a thing. So it has proved, for few places are harder to reach than the realm of the Halathrin, yet still from there the other half was taken."

"Can we reach and destroy the half you have hidden?"

"We must!" Aranloth said with sudden fierceness. "Or else Cardoroth will fall to sorcery. I, and the other lòhrens, cannot hold the elùgroths off forever. But the reaching of it is the problem."

"Why?"

Aranloth turned away. "Let me think. But first, before I decide anything, the king must learn of this. And in the choices that follow he also will have a hand."

Aranloth recalled the soldiers, and they filed up once more on the battlements, oblivious to what had transpired there. Had they known, they would have shown greater fear. But Brand knew; indeed he knew better than most just how powerful Shurilgar was and that, though the lòhren had expected to discover some artefact that enhanced the elùgroths power, this was a thing greater and darker than he had dreamed.

They made their way back to the palace with little speech. The lòhren remained deep in thought, and Brand studied the city as he rode. He looked at it now in a different light, for it was always that way when something was at risk.

The people showed little worry at the siege. They had endured such trials before and they trusted the high wall, and the skill of Gilhain, to save them. Brand was not so sure. The enemy was vast. They were led by foes determined to bring the city down, and treachery bred in Cardoroth like shadows in a dark forest. It was everywhere, else there would be less need for the Durlin. And on top of it all there was the sorcery to consider. No, there was good reason for fear, but not despair. While Gilhain drew breath, the city might survive, and there were others to help him.

The hooves of their horses clattered in the palace yard and they gave their horses to the stable boys to brush down and care for.

Aranloth hastened, striding up stairs and along corridors until at length they came to the king's chamber. The Durlin guards were not there, but a maid was just then coming out of the room.

"Is the king inside?" Aranloth asked.

She curtsied. "No, My Lord. The king left some while ago."

"Where is he then?"

"In council with the army commanders. At least so I heard the queen say to someone else."

Aranloth strode away. He turned as he went, speaking over his shoulder, "Thank you," he said.

The maid smiled and gave another curtsy.

Brand followed swiftly. There was not far to go, however. Aranloth guessed rightly which meeting chamber was being used and in moments he stood before the great doors. They were closed, and outside waited six Durlin, two more than usual.

They gave Brand the Durlin salute, a clenched fist over their hearts. He returned it, wondering if even six guards was enough, yet the men must take turns and rest. No one could stay alert all the time. Without rest they were useless, and the palace was the safest, though not *safe*, place in the city.

"Open the door," Brand commanded.

Two of the men obeyed. One gave a knock to the timber, using a brass weight that was set in the middle of the door so that those inside knew when an interruption was coming and not to utter any secrets until it was established who was entering.

Then both men swung the door open. It was a heavy contraption of oak, carved, decorated and paneled with gold. They entered, Brand allowing the lòhren to go first, for he was of higher standing in the city.

The lòhren stood in the doorway, and his face was grim. The captains looked at him. Lornach who sat next to the king, ready to protect him and summon the Durlin if trouble started inside the chamber, studied him also. And the king scrutinized them both, his eyes curious, knowing whence they had come from and what had been his task.

"I would speak with the king," Aranloth said.

Gilhain nodded, and his gaze shifted for a moment to the captains.

"Alone," Aranloth said. "Except for Brand."

Brand had not expected to be included in the discussion. He was not a counselor to the king, but his guard, and it seemed that the captains thought it strange also. But they did not like his ascension to the position of Durlindrath. They did not like *him*, because he was a foreigner, no matter that he had proved himself more than they had. But the king knew, and that was all that counted.

The soldiers filed out, annoyed to be dismissed, more annoyed that Brand was going in. They did not look at him or greet him as they passed.

Lornach was the last to go. He rolled his eyes as he neared, and Brand repressed a smile.

"Come in and take a seat. Tell me what you discovered," the king said to them.

They sat, but it was the king who spoke first.

"So, is it good news or bad?"

Aranloth leaned his staff against the edge of the table, but he did not let it go.

"The worst," the lòhren said.

Gilhain gave no reaction. If anything, the wolfish intelligence on his face showed just that little bit more determination.

"Tell me all," he said.

It did not take long. The king was familiar with Shurilgar; it would be hard to find someone who was not. The breaking of the staff and the hiding of the two pieces were all that was really new to him.

41

"And you're sure that it was the Halathrin piece that has somehow been found and taken?"

"I'm sure."

"The Halathrin will have guarded this thing well, no doubt. And its loss will devastate them. But so too will the fact that through them a great evil has been unleashed upon Alithoras. I wonder," Gilhain said, "if they would try to retrieve the thing. I cannot help but feel that they will. Perhaps they'll even send an army. That may be the chance that we're looking for, the one turn of events that could save us."

Aranloth sighed and let go of his staff. "O king," he said. "I wish that it would be so, but it will not. The Halathrin no longer venture into the lands beyond their forest realm. They suffered greatly, as you know, in the Elù-haraken, the Shadowed Wars. The immortals died like wheat before the scythe, though in numbers far less than men. Since those times they have become reclusive. There will be no army, but *perhaps* they will send a small group of their best to try to retrieve the staff. If so, when they discover that it is held in the midst of an army, they will give up. There will be no help from them, for they will bide their time and hope to retrieve it one day in the future when the guard is not so great. They are, after all, immortal. They have great patience to wait for such things."

"Then there's little hope for us. The elug army is patient too, and it will wear us down even if it takes another year. And no aid will come from anywhere else in Alithoras. Other cities are far away, and they stand in peril of invasion also. We must prepare ourselves for the long defeat. We knew it would come one day."

Aranloth held up his hand. "O king. You spoke of a last chance for Cardoroth. It will not be the Halathrin as

42

you hoped. Yet there *is* a chance, faint and slim. The last chance, and yet the best."

Gilhain looked at him. The wolfish intelligence of his eyes flashed.

"What chance is this? It's something new, and something to do with magic or sorcery rather than soldiers and swords, else we would have discussed it before now."

"So it is," Aranloth said. "For in every power there is a weakness. In every loss an opportunity. It is so with Shurilgar's staff. I said that the enemy has the one half. The other is not in their possession. But both are linked by the power that Shurilgar put into them. Should the second half be found, should it be destroyed, then the first will lose its potency. The power will drain from it. Perhaps even the timber itself will crumble to dust. I hope not for the latter, for I would return it to the Halathrin, yet I fear that such will be the case."

Gilhain looked at him shrewdly. "You say *if* it is found. Yet I guess that you already know where it is. Is that not so."

"That is so. Finding it will not be a problem. Retrieving it from the place in which it is hidden is where the difficulty lies. For if the Halathrin realm is well guarded, then the place where the second half is kept is warded by protections greater than all other places in Alithoras. The hope of success is so slight as to be barely there."

"And yet," said the king with his usual quick shrewdness, "if it was placed there for safekeeping, then it is possible to enter there again."

Aranloth nodded, but his face was grim, and his eyes held doubt.

Brand leaned forward. "It's time to reveal this hiding place of the second fragment. It cannot be *that* bad."

"It is worse. Worse than you could know. For it is hidden in the tombs of the Letharn."

Brand had not heard the name before. It meant nothing to him, but Gilhain sat back in his chair, a thoughtful expression on his face.

"There is a rumor, he said, "come down out of the ancient past about a people called the Letharn. Once they were mighty, the whisper says, yet their empire fell and now nothing remains of them. Are the tombs something to do with them?"

"Yes," Aranloth said. "It's to do with them, but saying they were mighty is like calling a massive old oak tree a splinter. Once, in an age so long ago that nothing is remembered save the tattered edges of legend, their empire stretched from the mountains of Auren Dennath in the north to the mountains of the Graèglin Dennath in the south. That is over three hundred leagues, and it reached inland in some places much further. But their empire fell before even the exodus of the Halathrin into these lands, and even the immortals found little more than traces of what once was great. And yet, some works of the Letharn remain, for not all that they achieved is lost."

The lòhren ceased talking, and his expression was pensive. But soon he put aside whatever he was thinking of and addressed them again.

"The tombs of the Letharn," he said, "are ancient. They began when their empire did, and the empire endured long before it fell. And in the noontide of their long rule the tombs were expanded, for ever they tunneled deeper into the hard rock of the earth where no light shines and few things live. And ever they needed more room. The wealth of nations was buried with their multitudinous dead, treasures that the cities of the Camar that came after could not match. If all that those cities owned for the last thousand years were piled into a hill, still it would seem as an ant mound to the mountains of wealth the Letharn gathered. But hold, O king, I see you look at me in amazement, and I see the light of desire in your eyes, for what person, be he king or no, would not want some share of that?"

The king shrugged. "The thought crossed my mind, but wealth is no good to Cardoroth if the city falls to the enemy. That is my only concern."

"And so it must stay," Aranloth said, "for the Letharn were a mighty people, and they were jealous of their wealth, and it does not lie unguarded…"

He turned now to Brand.

"Poison covers all the treasure from the least trinket to the most sacred of their heirlooms. It rests near those who once counted it, or wore in on finger, neck or head. Even in death they would keep it that way. Poison that you cannot see or smell covers all. That poison is so deadly, even after all this time, that whomsoever touches it dies a most dreadful death. And that is but the least protection. For in their noontide, the Letharn were a terrible people. Might they possessed of uncounted arms and never-defeated armies. Yet also among them were those who delved deep into lore that few understand. Other powers they had, greater than legions of soldiers. And they invoked them to guard the tombs."

Aranloth fell silent. Brand barely dared to ask, but he wanted to know something.

"What did the Letharn do?" he asked. "What powers did they raise to protect the tombs?"

"Something terrible," the lòhren answered. "A great feat of power, for they made three creatures, or rather they drew them forth from the very powers that form and substance the earth. And those creatures they set as guardians. They roam the tombs. Bound to them, they

45

cannot leave, and yet within them they are mighty. No lòhren, no elùgroth, not a hundred combined could stand against them."

The king looked at him intently. "Yet you must have ventured into those tombs, or else you could not have hidden the staff there."

Aranloth returned his gaze. "Yes, there is a way. The ancients created an enchantment, surpassing strong, yet they also created a way to circumvent it. The powers they called forth are called the harakgar. They are bound to the tombs, but they are not bound to any particular shape or form. There are three of them, and they always appear together in whatever guise they choose. And they do choose it, for they have intelligence as well as power. They cannot be slain – they can only be held off. There are words of power that lull them, but they only work to allow entry or exit from the tombs. Otherwise, the dead and their treasures could not have been laid to rest. Yet the words lose much of their strength should someone try to take a thing, howsoever small, away from the tombs. That, the harakgar do not tolerate, words no."

Brand ran his fingers through his hair. Sorcery and wizardry were all alike to him: he mistrusted anything that he could not hold and feel in his hand.

"Has *anything* ever been removed successfully from the tombs?"

"Yes," the lòhren said. He looked down at his staff as though remembering another time. "It was done with great cost, and luck, and I had others with me to help. Things could have easily gone awry."

"Then that gives me hope," Gilhain said. "If you have done it once, if you are willing to try again, then you might well succeed."

Aranloth laughed, but it was as though at a grim jest rather than with humor.

"There's only one problem with that," he said. "I cannot leave the city. Between me and the other lòhrens, we are just enough to hold the elùgroths at bay. Should one of us leave, you would be dead within the week. Should *I* leave, you would be dead within the day. No, O king, I wish to, but cannot undertake this quest."

Gilhain did not answer for a moment. There was silence while these words sunk in. At length, he glanced at the lòhren again.

"If neither you, nor another lòhren can go, then perhaps some other brave soul might attempt the deed?"

"That may be," Aranloth said. "Yet it would be a brave soul indeed, for while the words of power may be learned, as even any lòhren on the wall would need to be taught them, even one of them would likely die. It takes more than magic to survive in that place. To ask such a thing of a person without a lòhren's training, without their power, is to ask them to risk their lives for less than the slimmest chance of success. I say this to you truly, not even an army would suffice to fulfil this task, even if you could spare the men. The many can die just as easily as the few, and the way in the tombs is long and dark. It takes a certain kind of courage that few possess, perhaps only one in an army of ten thousand men, and then luck besides. Make no mistake. Words or no, the harakgar do not permit anything to leave the tombs: not a diamond as big as your fist nor a fragment of broken pottery. The words alone will not be enough."

Gilhain shook his head. "Then we're caught in a dilemma without hope."

Aranloth let out a long sigh. "In a dark place yes, but not totally void of hope. There might yet be a way, but if it is attempted, it will likely mean death to the person who goes, and certainly it will leave me with reduced power just when I need it most."

"What is this way then?" Gilhain asked. "For it's death to carry on as we are. We all know that."

5. The Fate of the Kingdom

Aranloth did not answer straightaway. It seemed as though he still debated something within his own mind, and this troubled Brand more than anything, for the lòhren was usually swift to assess a situation and to make a decision.

"If I cannot go, but someone *must* go, then we have to choose a person to go in my stead – if we can find anyone willing. As I said, in such a quest one person might avail as well as an army, for it's not by mere numbers or swords or courage, but rather by strength of will that the harakgar can be survived, and the quest be accomplished, if it can be accomplished at all." He leaned back in his chair, sifting through lore in his mind that Brand guessed few, if any, in Alithoras possessed.

"And the harakgar are not the only danger," he continued. "The enemy beyond our walls is cunning. Those who command know that I have learned of the staff. They will guess my next move – to seek to break the second half in order to reduce their power, and they will be watching. The breaking of the staff is their greatest fear, not only because it will undermine their power here, but because they hope one day to recover it. If both halves are drawn together again their power would be increased. And the elùgroths' hope is my fear."

He seemed as though he would say more of that, of the intentions of the enemy, but instead he carried on with things directly at hand. It did not matter, for Brand knew as well as everybody what the elùgroths and the armies that they commanded sought: the total domination of all of Alithoras.

"One alone, or a very small group," Aranloth continued, "might slip away from the siege and avoid the watchfulness of the enemy. Even so, it would take much luck, and there will be need of magic ere the end to face the harakgar if the person gets that far."

Gilhain sat back and crossed his arms. "But you said yourself that you cannot go, and neither can any of the lòhrens. So, there is no one with the skills that you require."

Aranloth pursed his lips. "There is no one with the skills. And yet even an unskilled person can wield a lòhren's staff as a weapon. To be sure, they could only summon a fragment of the power that a lòhren might, for most of a lòhren's power comes ultimately from inside themselves and not the staff. But when a staff is used the magic takes hold of it, becomes infused into the wood, and has a life of its own. That residual power is only a small help, but on such small chances, and what a person makes of them, often rests life and death, success and failure."

The king was thoughtful. "Such a person would have to be special. Their courage, wit and luck must be unmatched."

"So it must be," Aranloth said, exchanging a veiled glance with Gilhain, "for the fate of the kingdom would be balanced on their life and every choice they made. It is a great burden, and I would trust few, if any, to bear it."

"I also," Gilhain said. "Yet there is one in my realm who has proven their resourcefulness. One who has shown loyalty beyond question. And one that luck favors. So far, anyway."

"Who?" Brand asked. There were several he could think of that might match that description. Lornach seemed the most likely. But he did not wish to see his friend go on such a dangerous quest, nor did he wish to lose one of his best Durlin at a time when they were needed most.

There was a long silence. Aranloth looked at him with his typical gaze: eyes that had seen a thousand tragedies. The king looked at him with his usual wolfish keenness. For a while Brand did not understand, and then he realized that they were talking about him.

"You can't be serious," he said in a low voice.

"We're deadly serious," Gilhain said.

"But I have no powers against sorcery, and no affinity for magic. Aranloth's staff would be nothing more than an ordinary weapon in my hands."

"I will teach you the words needed to subdue the harakgar," Aranloth said. "And the staff will respond to your touch. It will give something of its powers, though how much and in what form I cannot say."

"You said yourself that those powers would not be enough. You said that even a lòhren might not have the strength to escape the creatures in the tombs."

"I said that other virtues are needed also. Virtues that anyone could have, though few do, whether they're lòhrens or not. You have those qualities," he paused, his expression thoughtful, "and maybe you will surprise yourself if you use the staff in need. It will be more than a prop for tired legs. You will be able to tap into something that few others could, and in truth, if I cannot go, only you would I trust in my stead. I will give my staff to no other. Nor would I trust such a quest to anybody else."

Brand hesitantly reached out, looking at the same time into Aranloth's eyes for permission, and took the staff in his hand. It felt comfortable and balanced in his grip. He put it down again.

"It feels good in my hand, but as a weapon of timber and nothing else. I don't lightly say no to you, Aranloth. You've helped me so much. Your counsels are always dark, but profitable. But I *must* say no. As you trust no one else for this quest, neither do I trust anyone else to guard the king. Not as I do. I cannot go."

Gilhain stirred. "And if I, as your king, command you, will you not then go?"

"No," Brand said without hesitation. "My place is by your side."

The king gave his wolfish grin. It was not the reaction Brand expected.

"Well, I will not command you," he said. "Even kings do not lightly order those who serve them to face likely death. And yet I say this to you. Well have you guarded me. But time is running out. Not even you can protect me forever. If the staff isn't destroyed, Cardoroth will surely fall. It may well fall anyway, but the outcome is then less certain. These are facts. If you would protect me, you *must* take up this quest, but you should go of your own free will, though with my blessing. If not, then you shall stay, and we will die and fight the great dark together when it comes for us. What do you say?"

Brand did not answer. He knew it was death to stay, death if the power of the elùgroths was not broken. But this strange quest, to a place that he did not know, there to pit himself against powers beyond him, that was death too.

In the silence that now held the room he heard from afar the sound of battle renewed at the walls. It was a dim echo of screams and clashes of arms, of hurtled missiles against the walls. In his mind he imagined the rush of the enemy, the swift flight of hissing arrows, the throwing up of ladders and knotted climbing ropes, and the death that followed. He had seen battle. He was expert at it, in all the ways to protect himself and kill an enemy. He had seen battle, and he did not like it. If nothing was done, he would see it one day in the streets, and then the palace, and then finally, if he was still alive, at bay somewhere with the king. He saw that in his mind also, and he did not like it either.

Brand bowed his head. Neither the king nor Aranloth spoke. At length, he sighed and looked at them again.

"I'll go," he said. "Though I see little hope in it, yet it is better than the certainty of defeat."

Gilhain straightened. A strange look came over him. It was one of hope renewed.

"Against the raging swords of the enemy who would bring darkness," the king said, "you shall be a sword of light! You are the one hope that we set against many despairs. You are become Cardoroth's champion in her darkest hour."

Brand slowly shook his head. "But I wasn't even born here. Many in the city would be happy to see me leave and never return. It may be Cardoroth's darkest hour, but I'm not her champion. The men on the walls who defend us each day, they are each and every one of them Cardoroth's champions."

The king rested a hand on his shoulder. "Many begrudge your rise in my service. You're a foreigner, and they do not like that. You are young, and they do not like that either, but I read the people of the city better than you do. This is truly our hour of deepest peril, and as king and guardian of each and every life in this realm, I choose *you* for our hope. And should you return to this city, should it still stand, you will see that there is more love for you here than you think."

Brand was not so sure about that. He knew that the people he dealt with on a daily basis, the lords of the realm and the commanders of the army, had little love for him. They begrudged the respect the king showed him, and they would prefer that one of their own received it instead of what they considered a wild man from the tribes of the Duthenor. And yet the ordinary people seemed to like him. For the king, and for them, he would do his best to live up to Gilhain's hopes.

"Let's assume I can retrieve this broken staff," he said, turning to Aranloth. "It's a thing of power. I have seen the one half, and it's filled with sorcery. How can such a powerful artifact be destroyed?

6. A Chance at Life

Aranloth shrugged. "Sometimes you over think things. The staff is made of timber – it'll burn."

The lòhren looked at Brand with sudden intensity after his casual words. "But you must remember this at all cost. Do *not* destroy the staff within the tombs. It will enrage the harakgar beyond any hope of escape. Their sole purpose, their very reason for existence, is to protect all that is laid to rest there. If you reach the outside again, that is the place to start a fire. The harakgar are bound to the tombs. They cannot take one step beyond them, and nor should you until the staff is destroyed, for the elùgroths must *not* have a chance to reclaim it."

"None of this is going to be easy, I suppose," Brand said.

"Not much in life ever is," Aranloth replied. "Listen though!" he said. "I will teach you the words that might make it possible. Without them you will die. With them, you might lull the harakgar's powers just enough for your other talents to make the difference between life and death."

The lòhren leaned in close and whispered. He said words in a foreign tongue, harsh and strange. Brand guessed it was the very language of the Letharn themselves, a tongue now dead, unspoken by all except Aranloth and those like him. Though it would not surprise Brand if Aranloth, alone in all the many lands of Alithoras, knew this lore.

When he was done the lòhren leaned back and stared into his eyes.

"Burn those words into your mind. Forget them and you are a dead man."

Brand nodded. Having learned them, he would not forget. There were only two now who knew them, for so well kept was their secret that Aranloth had even whispered them in the presence of a king. But if Gilhain was offended, he did not show it.

Aranloth leaned in close again. "Whisper them back," he said.

Brand did so. He repeated them several times until the lòhren appeared satisfied.

"Do not forget!" he commanded. "Recite them when you wake. Recite them when you prepare for sleep. Make them flow through your mind like the blood that surges through your veins, or when you stand in the tombs you will be utterly defenseless against the harakgar, and sword and staff and even luck will avail you nothing. Do not forget!"

Brand had no intention of doing so, but he was surer of his sword as a weapon than any words. Yet he was not stupid, and the manner of the lòhren convinced him of their need.

"How shall I find my way to the staff?" he asked. "The tombs are vast, you say. It would be best to take the swiftest route."

Aranloth took up a quill left from the king's meeting with the army commanders.

"I'll draw you a map and teach you the way. It may be that necessity will drive you to venture a different path, either on the way in or out, so I'll include several. There are many however – the ways of the tombs are myriad. And it's a dark place, full of fear and nameless things. Don't stray from my paths, or else you'll wander in there, alone in the dark, until you lay yourself down to die among the already dead."

Brand watched as the lòhren drew the map and offered instructions and descriptions of the various things he would see. He memorized this also, for he trusted better to his memory of the lòhren's words than to a map. He noticed as well that he drew this in front of the king, and that Gilhain listened with interest. Brand supposed the map was useless without the words to lull the harakgar, and that reaffirmed for him their importance. Still, even the sendings of the elùgroths had proved vulnerable to a blade, and he guessed that the harakgar would be put to the same test. In steel he trusted rather than magic, and it had never let him down yet.

"So much for the tombs," Aranloth said. "But you must get there first for any of this to matter. Before you came to Cardoroth you wandered in the wild lands. But you never went far to the south?"

"No. I crossed the Careth Nien, the Great River, far to its north when it was ice-bound. I wandered in the shadow of the mountains to the north, for something there lured me, but the winter bit cold, and I was pursued at the time, so I headed south to warmer climes and Cardoroth, rumor of which has reached even the Duthenor."

"Well, from here," the lòhren said, "you must journey due south. It's some fifty leagues or more to another river, this time the Carist Nien. When you reach its banks turn east and follow it to the land of the Angle that I described. That is the place where the river splits in two. You'll not miss it. The waterfall there, and other things, are remarkable. That is a journey nearly as far as the first leg. In all it's some three hundred miles. A long way to travel on foot, but there's no way to take a horse out of the city. If you would shorten the journey, you must find a mount on the way, if you can. But the lands all about are controlled by the enemy, though no doubt most are with this army that besieges us. You'll not find help along the way, but I can't rule it out altogether, for there are other strongholds that resist the enemy. But they are along the coast – too far east for you to go. Still, the lands are wild and much may happen between here and the Angle."

"Clearly there's a way to escape this siege, albeit without a horse," Brand said. "Where is it?"

"We'll meet at dusk at the West Gate. From there, we'll show you the way."

"But the enemy is most heavily concentrated on our western wall, and the Angle is to the south."

"That may be," the king said. "But the only way out lies westward."

Brand did not like it. Westward lay the shadow-haunted pine forests around Lake Alithorin. He had been inside them, more than once, and he was not keen to go back. Every time he went there he came near to death.

"For now," the king continued, "we have said all that can be said and made what decisions that could be made. It's best for you to rest. Prepare what equipment and food you would take, though it cannot be much while traveling on foot, and then rest while you can until dusk. It'll be a long night, and you'll be glad of some sleep now when the time for escape comes later.

Brand stood up. The king shook his hand.

"This is no easy task we have set you," Gilhain said, "but do not think that either I or Aranloth would send you if we did not trust in the fact that you might achieve it. And if the worst happens, for either of us, then know this. From the wild lands you came to us, young, brash, confident – and a complete stranger. You leave now as Cardoroth's champion, and the friend of the king. Fare well, and if we do not meet again, know that nothing lasts forever. So my people often say, but we say also this: the sun is warm when it shines, and memories endure a lifetime."

Brand did not answer. But he gripped the king's arm in the warrior's handshake, and then turned and left. But from the doorway he spoke again.

"We'll meet again, Gilhain," he said quietly. "I swore an oath to protect you, and I fulfil it now in a strange way. So are the turns of fortune. But I think I'll return to this city, and to you, my king. When I do, we shall share our stories, for I think we'll both have much to tell."

Gilhain turned to the lòhren when Brand had gone.

"What fortune swept him into my realm?" he asked.

"I don't know, yet good fortune it was," Aranloth answered.

"Are all the Duthenor as he? If so, they will one day conquer the world."

Aranloth tilted his head at those last words as if in thought.

"Perhaps they could. But they are a fragmentary people at the moment. Once, one of Brand's ancestors united them. Someone could do so again, but they are not all like Brand. He is ... one of a kind. Cardoroth will not see his like again."

Gilhain let out a long breath. "I hope he returns. I don't doubt that we made the right choice, for in him is our hope, and there is no other. I would bet on him. In fact, I *have* bet on him, and the stake is all our lives."

"He is our one hope," Aranloth agreed. "But he does not yet fully understand the peril of the task that we have set him. Yet if he did, he would still attempt it. Once he has made up his mind his determination builds. Normal people suffer setbacks, and he will be sure to endure many, but with them it weakens resolve. In his case, ill fortune strengthens his will instead."

"That's true," the king said. "Yet do you wonder if the task we set him is beyond accomplishment? Truly, what do you think his chances are? You know much of these tombs, while he and I know nothing."

Aranloth drummed the fingers of one hand along his staff.

"I would not send him if I did not think it could be done. Much will depend on the workings of his mind, for it is to that, and that alone, that the power in my staff will respond." The lòhren paused, as if trying to find the right words. "Magic is not made from nothing. It's a transformation of all the forces around us, a transformation inspired by the mind of a person. No magic is ever quite the same as another, for no minds are ever truly alike. What he will get from the staff, and what the staff will get from him, I cannot guess. But for all his words that he mistrusts magic, he has a greater connection to it than he knows. At least I think so, and for that we must hope, or he will not return."

"So," Gilhain said. "Even as I bet our lives on his courage, you have bet our lives that he will be able to use the magic of your staff. But you did not really answer my question. What do you think his chances are?"

"They're not good," Aranloth said. "We all know that. If I had to put a number on it, I would say perhaps one chance in a hundred, but it's the only chance we have. He'll also need luck. But he's a lucky man."

"In my experience," Gilhain said, "a man makes his own luck."

"That's true. It's a truth better realized by the old than the young, for life is also like magic. It's not made from nothing, but is a transformation of all the forces around us. But the mind has the greatest influence. Even so, there are other powers in this world besides courage and magic and determination. Men like Brand attract them, and their fates are woven through with the inexplicable. Call it fate if you will, or fortune, or luck. But whatever name you put to it, it gathers round him. That much I knew from the first time we met."

"Ah," Gilhain said. "It seems long ago now, for much has happened since then. But he is still young. *Too* young many of my advisors say. But they don't understand. In him I trust. He's never let me down, and I in turn will never let *him* down. He has become as dear to me as the son that I lost."

Aranloth sighed. "You love him, as I have also learned to do."

"Yes, and though it seems that I sent him now into great peril, it may be that he has the most chance to live, for he will escape the city. He might survive what comes after, for though it will not have occurred to him just yet, he will realize sooner or later that if the harakgar press him too hard he might live by dropping Shurilgar's staff and leaving it in the tombs."

"That is so," Aranloth said.

"It might be better that way. For I would be glad if he lived. And he would be glad to return to the lands of the Duthenor. He only stays here to help me. Otherwise he would have gone back before now. That is where his destiny is, if there is such a thing, and there he would be spared from Cardoroth's fall, as we will not. I would have it so."

"Perhaps," Aranloth said. "But his destiny with the Duthenor is linked to his destiny in Cardoroth. He's not quite ready yet for what will follow if he returns to his home. There is more for him to learn before he can face those problems – and his enemies."

Gilhain gave a wan smile. "What man is ever ready for such things?"

Aranloth acknowledged his words with a solemn inclination of his head. For a long while after, they sat in silence.

7. A Token of Trust

Night crept through the streets of Cardoroth. It came slowly, spreading shadows before it that filled the narrow alleys first.

The last rays of the sun gleamed off golden domes and then shot up into the sky to spark the first shimmering of stars. Then the darkness came. Swift it fell, as though a lamp were snuffed out, and the air stilled, and an eerie silence grew. This was no rowdy city; not tonight. It was a city under siege, and word of the dark sorcery of the previous night ran from district to district, house to house, person to person. Fear ruled the shadows tonight. The house doors were shut. The inns were empty. All the city's windows were barred.

Brand rode slowly through the streets. He enjoyed the quiet. It gave him a chance to think and to prepare himself for what was coming. He was not nervous, not yet. That would come later. But he had experienced nerves before. He acknowledged them, as always, for a man void of nerves was a man oblivious to danger, and that was a danger in itself. So, when the nerves did come, and they would, he knew how to deal with them. What froze others set his true spirit free, for was he not a wild man of the Duthenor after all? And these city folk, guarded by walls, the strategies of a great king, soldiers and laws, they did not understand that in life-and-death struggles all their wealth and privileges and culture counted for nothing. There was only strength of will.

He had put away the white surcoat of the Durlin. But the chain mail the king had given him, light yet strong, whispered reassuringly to him beneath the drab tunic he now wore.

He arrived at the West Gate and found the king already there. Aranloth was with him, and also Taingern and Lornach and every surviving member of the Durlin.

He had not expected that. Rather, he had intended to slip away unseen and unknown, for farewells were hard, and he had said more than he wished to in his short life. Nor was there any need to give his two lieutenants any instructions. Both of them knew their task.

There were few others about. Only those who needed to be abroad had ventured the streets this night. For the most part they were soldiers, and though they must guess that something was happening, they did not know what.

Finding a hitching rail, he tied his horse. The black stallion was his favorite, and he wished he could ride him on this quest. He would have been more than company on a lonely road; his was a bold heart that showed no fear, and it gave of its strength without stint. The horse could run all day and still finish with a burst of speed.

He ran his hands along its flanks and over its head. "I'll be back," he said, "And when the enemy is gone, I'll take you for a long ride where the grass is green and the water cool and fresh."

The horse tossed its head and neighed. Brand gave it a last pat and turned to face the others.

Lornach and Taingern had approached. If ever there were two people the complete opposite of each other it was these. One was tall and courteous as a king of old; one was short and irreverent. Yet they both had this in common: they were his friends.

Taingern shook his hand in the warrior's grip. "Take care," he said with quiet intensity.

Lornach took his hand in the same fierce grip. "We don't know exactly what your quest is," he said, "But we know this much. You're going to light a bonfire under the pimply backsides of those pasty-faced sorcerers. So, best of luck! We all want to see that."

Brand flashed them both a grin. "I'd like to see it too. The fire part anyway."

They said no farewells, and neither did he. They pretended he would return, and he went along with that. But they all knew this was likely their last meeting, and the hard held warrior's grip said more than their words.

The gathered Durlin saluted him as he walked past, fists to heart, and then their swords leapt from their sheaths and flashed high above their heads catching the gleam of flickering torches near the gate.

Brand drew his own blade, the sword of his forefathers that had passed down from chieftain to chieftain of the Duthenor through years uncounted. Slowly, he kissed the metal, and then softly but clearly he voiced the Durlin creed:

Tum del conar – El dar tum!
Death or infamy – I choose death!

The Durlin gave a cheer, and then sheathed their blades. The city was quiet again, and Brand moved through the ranks of his men until he came to the king and the lòhren standing within the light of the gate torches.

"The time is nearly upon us," Gilhain said. "The evening grows dark, and the enemy is settling down for another night. But before you go, we have some gifts for you. May they help you on the road."

Aranloth stepped forward. He held the lòhren staff in his hand. "This I give to you until we meet again. You will find it useful at need. Trust in it, as I trust in you, and you will draw more from it than you guess."

65

Brand took it. He had never heard tell of a lòhren parting with their staff, but what Aranloth did next surprised him more.

With steady hands the old man reached up and carefully took the diadem from his head. It was a delicate thing of silver, plain and yet beautiful. Most of the time Brand never even saw it, but he knew that sometimes it flickered with its own light when the lòhren put forth his power.

Brand was not sure what to do. He did not want anything to do with magic. The staff and the diadem would be useless to him, and yet the lòhren kept no trinkets and would offer nothing without purpose. So, Brand removed his helm, the horned helm of the Duthenor that their enemies had learned to hate, and allowed the lòhren to place the diadem on his head. The silver centerpiece came to rest on his forehead. It was so light, and fitted so well, that he barely felt it there, but it was cool against his skin and there was something about it that seemed calming.

He put the helm back on, covering it. "Two gifts," he said to the lòhren, "and I know they are not lightly given. I will care for them as best as fate and chance allow, and return them if I may."

Aranloth gave a bow. "You will need them – more than you think. Remember most of all the harakgar charm that I taught you, and between the three things you might yet return. If it helps, I think you will."

Brand glanced at him sharply.

"Nay," the lòhren said. "I have not had a vision, and I offer no foretelling. Call it wishful thinking if you will. Or call it trust. But the words are no more lightly given than the gifts."

"Thank you, Aranloth," Brand said, "I fear that my skill lies in blades and the art of war, and that the virtues of staff and diadem will prove beyond my reach. I have no desire for magic and mistrust it, but time shall tell its own tale."

Aranloth gazed at him intently. "I would give you neither gifts if they would not turn to some benefit in your possession. And you mistrust magic, you say? Then you are already wiser in its ways than many who possess it and use it daily. But as you say, time shall tell its own tale."

The lòhren stepped back a little, and Gilhain came closer. He drew from the pocket of his robe a sheathed knife.

"This," the king stated, "is said to have come down through my line from the days of old, even from Carnhaina, that great queen of my people. It has no special value, or none that I know of save for its great antiquity and that her hands once held the hilt, but it's believed that it brings luck to all of our line. So it has proved for me since first my father gave it to me. May it prove so for you, and yours. If nothing else, it will be a sharp knife in the wild."

Brand bowed low. He looked carefully at the hilt and the sheath. It was Halathrin made, of that he was certain, though he had never seen their workmanship except for his own sword and the helm he wore.

The hilt was decorated with a strange design. Two small gems gleamed in the dim light, the sign of the Lost Huntress, the constellation of Halathgar. It was the same design as on the ring he wore on his finger, a gift itself after saving the great queen's tomb from ransacking. Well did he believe that once she had owned this thing.

He took the knife, drew it, and held it before him. He liked it. It felt good in his hand. But the king's words reminded him that he was not married nor likely to continue his own line.

"No," he said. "I cannot accept this. It's too kingly a gift, and a thing of your own family. Most especially, it brings you luck, which surely you need more than me. You'll be hard pressed while I'm gone, each and every day without stint."

He tried to hand it back, but Gilhain would not take it.

"We both need it," the king said. "But only one can have it. Accept it from me as a token of my trust in you. You cannot gainsay a gift of your king. It's mine to give, and I give it to you."

Brand could not refuse. It was a great gift, and one of more than knife alone. It would be churlish not to accept. He bowed again, deeply, but found no words to say. He was humbled.

Next, the king drew forth a great diamond, large as a child's fist, from his robes. It glittered in the torchlight, catching the dancing flames on its many surfaces and throwing the light back with a shimmer.

"This is no ancient thing," Gilhain said, "Nor is it an heirloom of my house. But it is of value, and you will find it so wherever you travel among Camar or Duthenor or further lands still that kings of the east know not, but perhaps the wandering feet of a bold man might tread. I give it to you, for you may survive, even if Cardoroth falls, and then I would ensure you had money to support yourself and to further your aims among the Duthenor when the time is right for your return to them."

Brand grinned at him. "Another kingly gift! But if I come not back here, then I am dead."

"That may be," Gilhain answered. "But not even a king knows what road he will walk until his feet are upon it. Take it on the chance that you survive and Cardoroth does not. For despite all our efforts, so it might come to pass, and I would not have one that earned such great reward leave my service without a token of recompense."

Brand took the diamond. It was no token. He suspected it was worth a king's ransom, yet the knife was still the greater gift.

Aranloth led them through a side door into the base of the tower. It was dark inside, the torches meant to burn in here were extinguished.

They went down a flight of stairs, near stumbling in the dark, but halfway down beyond sight of the entry a soft light sprang from the tip of Aranloth's staff.

The Durlin did not follow them. They were alone, and the noise of the city, such as it was, was dimmed to a far distant mutter.

There was nothing in the basement of the tower save an old rug and a table and chairs. All was covered in dust, but the furniture had recently been moved and the rug exposed.

Aranloth bent and pulled it aside. The stone floor was revealed, and set within it was a small wooden trapdoor. This was the secret exit from the city.

The king himself took hold of the brass ring in the timber and opened it, exposing a rickety ladder that descended into the dark.

"I thought I knew this tower," Brand said. "But this was under my nose for quite a while, and I never knew it."

"Cardoroth is an old city," the king answered. "It has many secrets, and even I don't know them all. But don't be dismayed that you worked here for a while and didn't know. Few do. It's well hidden and better guarded."

They walked along a narrow passage. It was a confined place, hung with webs, covered in dust, and it showed no sign that anybody had ventured here in hundreds of years. Ahead, the tunnel came to an abrupt end.

Brand looked around. The stone was bare of ornament or sign. There was no opening, at least none that he could see, but the king pushed at a certain place on the far wall, and the stone turned at his touch like a door. And so it was, for at once he saw hinges recessed with skill and precision, and that what he had taken to be stone was in fact heavy timber painted by some art to look like the other walls in the tunnel.

They moved through the door. On the other side were two guards. They did not speak, evidently having been prepared for tonight's unusual events at some earlier time.

Before the guards was a strong metal gate, a replica of the grand gate above, though much smaller. Yet it was strong, and obviously whoever had had this built did not rely on secrecy alone to protect the city from any chance that the enemy should discover this route and attempt to use it.

Gilhain produced an ornate key. With a click and a rattle he opened the gate and they walked through. The way was now a little wider, but the guards did not follow them.

There were six more gates. Each guarded, though now by lone soldiers. A bell was at each station to provide advance warning should some enemy try to break through.

Brand wondered why the tunnel was wider than at its beginning. It did not really make any sense, but then he noticed the pillars that studded each side. A long chain was attached to each and ran the length of the tunnel. He guessed this was another defense. At need the tunnel could be collapsed, thus preventing entry into the city but also killing, in mass, whoever was attempting to force their way inside.

They came to the last gate after what seemed nearly an hour of travel, though it was hard to tell in their strange surrounds. At a sign from the king the guard there withdrew.

"This is it," Gilhain said. "The last gate. From here your quest begins."

"And your danger," added Aranloth.

"The one goes with the other," Brand said. "But we all knew that from the beginning." He paused, and then took the king's hand in the warrior's grip, even as he had done with the Durlin.

"Stay safe until I come back," he said.

"And you also," Gilhain answered. "We'll await your return, for if you're successful it'll tip the advantage back to us. I don't think Cardoroth will remain besieged if the enemy suffers such a defeat. But if you're not successful, there are other choices than death, whatever the Durlin creed says. A man can only do so much. Fate shoulders the rest. If you can, live well off the diamond, and, maybe, you can reclaim your rightful place among the Duthenor."

"It's better," Brand said, "to serve a great king than to lead a small people. I'll return."

Aranloth shook his hand. "Don't forget that a small people can become a great one. But fate will be what it will be," he said. "Good luck, and may the sun ever rise on your face and set at your back."

They spoke no more. Brand moved down the shadowed passage, leaving behind two that he loved and a city that had become home.

The passageway swiftly narrowed. It became dark, wet and dirty. At times he had to crawl, worming his way forward, but at length he felt the whisper of fresher air and the sounds of nightlife. The rough floor now turned at an upward slope, and he climbed slowly; not because of the rough passageway, but because he did not know with certainty what lay at the end of the path. And that was near.

Crawling on his belly he neared the exit. It was only a crack in the rock; whether natural, or man-made and given the appearance of something natural, he could not tell.

He listened and looked from within the last foot of the tunnel, but it was too dark to see much, and he could not hear anything out of place. He crept further forward, and his head now stuck out. He could see a little better and discovered that he was somewhere amid piled and tumbled rocks on what seemed to be a steep hill.

With drawn sword he climbed out, but there seemed no cause for alarm. Yet his life among the Duthenor, where he had been hunted for many years by his enemies, and his trials in Cardoroth, had taught him caution.

He saw ahead of him that the slope rose to cliffs, but there was a path, barely perceptible, that led up to the top of the hill by a less steep route. This he took, and then looked out on the night-darkened lands below.

Cardoroth was there, the great city itself alight with a glow from tens of thousands of windows. It was still, but before it was great movement. On the flat lands near the west wall he saw the shadowy mass of the enemy, lit by their cooking fires, seething and roiling with movement for the evening meal was being taken after the long fighting of the day.

But even for this time of day there seemed too much movement, as though they were in disarray or some strange event had occurred in their camp. This was confirmed when he heard the wild blast of a horn. It was no call to end hostilities for the day or to signal the movement of troops to sentry positions: it was an alarm. But for what?

It was a question that disturbed him, and he did not like the feel of things. Something was wrong.

But what? He studied the activity below as best as the darkness allowed. There was certainly a movement of troops, though it appeared disorderly. It was possible the enemy was sending out some sort of patrol. If so, it was a large one, and it was coming in his direction.

Could they possibly know that he was here? He could see no way that they would, although Aranloth had said they would anticipate the move. Yet they could not know in what direction the attempt to escape the city would be made. Coincidence, or knowledgeable action? He could not decide, but the possibility that they knew of his movements could not be ruled out. There were traitors in the city, and they may well have a means of communicating with the enemy. He could have been seen. Guesses might have been made.

None of it mattered. Brand decided not to wait to find out what was going on. He had not liked the thought of the westward exit earlier, but now it pleased him, for the hill was in range of the pinewoods that surrounded Lake Alithorin. He knew those dreary woods, and though he did not like them they offered a great place to find concealment or lose any pursuit, so long as those who followed were not too numerous.

He moved back down the slope and toward the tree line. It was no accident that the exit was here. It was placed for the very purposes that he had used it for: to spy on the enemy and then to disappear. And yet he could not travel fast for he had no horse and his pack was laden with food.

The ground levelled. Rocks gave way to grassy earth, but the trees thickened around him swiftly, and soon he was lost in another world. The pine forest surrounding Lake Alithorin had a sinister reputation, and he knew better than most why. He paused as he entered its deep shadows, but from behind him the horn sounded again and he had no choice. He stepped forward, but he did so quietly and with his eyes wide open.

8. The Enemy is Everywhere

Brand looked up through the deepening tree canopy. He could no longer see the sky, and it was very dark. So dark that his pace was become slow, and that worried him. But should there be any kind of pursuit, the same problems that he was having would also hinder those who followed.

He moved ahead. The forest was quiet. The gray trunks of the pines rose like silent statues all about him. The fallen needles were soft beneath his boots, but there were many broken and rotting branches that he had to be careful of, and outthrust roots that turned and twisted in the dark as though to trip him. He ducked beneath a long trailer of moss that hung like a beard from a massive branch, and there he paused in mid-stride.

A sound drifted to him. Perhaps from close by, perhaps from far away; it was hard to tell amid all the trees. But wherever it came from, it was a wolf's howl, long and torturous, and it prickled the hair on the back of his neck.

When the long howl ceased the forest was left deadly quiet. He heard nothing save for his own breathing and the gentle trudge of his boots along the dim trail, if trail it even was. He could not see properly, yet he knew that he was headed deeper into the forest. Not a place that he wished to go, and yet if he persisted and passed through the timber the path would eventually lead to Lake Alithorin.

If the forest was an uncanny place, steeped in ancient tales and drenched with brooding menace, then the lake was its opposite. It was a place of beauty. Its pale shores were soft and sandy, surrounding a great basin of silver water alive with flashing fish, gently lapping waves and a sense of peace at odds with the dark forest around it. That was where he was headed, for it was safer there and he could turn south on its verge and follow it for many miles on the beginning of his quest.

But the forest was where he was at the moment, and he kept his mind on it instead of wandering too far ahead. There were noises now. The wolf was silent, but many small animals scurried in the deep shadows and near-noiseless wings beat over his head, passing shadows in the deeper shadows of the night.

And then he heard a different type of noise. It came from a distance, and it was not some small animal. It was the crashing through the woods of a great number of things, and he guessed what they were: elugs. He had little doubt of it, but then the horn sounded again, closer this time, and what uncertainty there was died even as its last urgent echoes were swallowed by the dark forest.

There was nothing to do but keep going, and this he did, but he moved at a swifter pace. Yet it was dangerous to move too fast in the dark and without due caution for what lay ahead. *Fire and blood!* This was not turning out as he expected. Or at least it was falling apart more quickly than he guessed.

Aranloth had warned him the enemy would be watching for such a move as he now made. But how could they possibly react so quickly? The more he thought of it the surer he was that some traitor had stumbled onto their plan, or at least a part of it, and the elùgroths did the rest.

It was beyond him how a person could betray their own city, and all the people in it. Yet where there was temptation of wealth, or power, or inducement by fear, all things were possible.

He decided to stop thinking about it. His best chance to get through the next few hours was to forget about everything behind him and move forward with a clear mind.

He was not skilled at tracking, or the hiding of his own trail. He was not skilled at hiding and finding concealment. He knew only what any hunter knew, or any herdsman of cattle and sheep, about trails, cover and hiding scent. But that knowledge would hardly serve against a host of enemies. What he did have in his favor were long legs and a willingness to endure the physical hardship of a desperate march. With luck, and the wild ways of the wood to help him, it might be enough.

It grew even darker, but there was no fog yet, and that was what he most hoped for. But fogs generally only rose from Lake Alithorin in the late hours of the night, and there were many miles he yet had to tread before he would benefit from that.

For many reasons his best course of action would be to head, as directly as the twisting trails through the trees allowed, to the shore of the lake. The closer he got, the thicker the fog would be, when, and if, it came. If necessary, shallow water would hide both scent and trail.

As a last resort he could also swim, something that he doubted the elugs could do with any proficiency, if at all. They came from desert lands, or at least the arid south of Alithoras. But that was truly a last resort, for the lake was massive, and strong as he was he would not endure long wearing mail and helm, nor survive any great length of time in its cold waters.

The night lengthened. The hours passed in sweat and toil and the taking of several false trails. Yet if he, who knew these woods was having difficulty, it would be worse for the elugs. Yet the noise of pursuit in the distance did not abate, though it drew no closer. But that noise was probably coming from the greater mass of those who followed. Ahead of the main group would be the fleeter footed, the stronger and the more eager for blood. It was a disturbing thought.

It was impossible to tell amid the trees and dark how close he was to the shore, but he knew now that he must be getting near. The ground often sloped a little downward, the trees grew thicker, the earth seemed lighter under foot as though there was sand in it. But there was no fog, nor yet even the first signs of one.

Suddenly, he burst through into the open. A white strand shimmered beneath the starlight of an open sky. Beyond the bright shore lay Lake Alithorin. It was, as ever, magnificent. But its beauty was not what attracted him now. He wanted water, for though he had a waterbag in his pack he had not yet drunk. That must last him through times when water was harder to find.

He moved to the shore carefully. There was no sign of anything about, but he was in the open now and it unsettled him. But nothing moved while he went forward, and reaching the water he knelt down and scooped up a double handful to drink. He studied his surrounds after a sip with the intensity of a shy deer, but everything seemed normal and he drank again.

He had nearly had his fill when he heard the elug horn blow again. It was closer this time, and then other horns answered it. They too were just as close, and they were not far from each other. The elugs did not seem to be throwing out a wide line and scouring the forest for him; rather they were on his direct trail, yet he had heard no dogs barking. How else could they track him other than by scent? Unless ... unless by sorcery.

The thought sent a chill through his body. But again, having come to the realization that such a thing was a possibility, he must not worry about it. Worry, anger and fear were his enemies as much as the elugs. He must concentrate only on himself and his next move.

It was time to turn south. If he stayed on the shore he could move much faster. There was more light, and there were no obstacles to swift walking or even running. Yet he would leave a trail that even a blind man could follow. Alternatively, he could ease back into the verge of trees and travel parallel to the lake. What was more important? Speed or concealment?

He chose speed. It seemed to him that it was useless to hide his trail. The enemy was already following him. His best chance now lay in outpacing them. He set off at a jog along the shore.

The sand was moist and firm beneath his boots. He moved at a good speed, and yet one that he could maintain for hours. He was less used to running than he once was, but the duties of Durlindrath kept him strong and fit.

Each day he trained with some of his men. They fought hand to hand, or used knives or spears or halberds. They fought with long swords and short, with staffs and daggers, with two-handed swords and one handed. Sometimes they trained with two swords, sometimes a sword and shield. They practiced archery, and they practiced defending against attack by arrow, spear or hurled dagger. They practiced everything.

None of this was new to him. He learned such things in his homeland. He had needed to, for he was hunted there by his enemies just as the king was a target now. But if he ever returned to the Duthenor, things would be different. He was older, more experienced. He was ready to claim back the life that was stolen from him.

The thought spurred him to jog a little faster. But at that moment he heard more noise in the forest. It was close, very close, and he stopped thinking about ever returning to his homeland and wondered instead if he would ever see another sunrise.

There was a greater clamor, and a sudden shout, but whether he had been seen or not he did not know. There seemed only one thing left to do: he must enter the water. He was a good swimmer, and that did not frighten him in itself, but he could not discard his sword or his chain mail. He would be weighed down and unable to swim, yet that did not mean that he could not find concealment somewhere in the shallows. Perhaps the search would sweep him by. If so, it would have to do so swiftly, for the water was fed by mountains and it was cold. Maybe dangerously cold for more than an hour.

He prepared to go in. His feet turned in that direction, but he had only taken a few strides when three elugs broke from the tree line ahead of him. They had bows, though no arrows were fitted to the strings. For a moment they did not see him, and then one gave a shout and the others looked. Their faces broke into hideous grins and they cried out in some harsh tongue. Answers came from all around and then there were horns. They blew and wailed and brayed, filling the forest with a ferocious din. The enemy was all around him.

A moment he hesitated. But the water was no longer an option. The three elugs were already drawing arrows from their quivers. He could not hide in the water, and being visible he would be easy prey for arrow shot. He must head back into the trees where their bows were useless and they had to fight him sword to sword. That, he might survive, if there were not too many of them.

He darted to the left and into the dark shadows of the trees. As he did so he heard more horns. These were so close that the sound of them hurt his ears and there was a great crashing in the timber nearby.

The enemy was everywhere. He drew his sword. The thought struck him that this would be the end. He had failed the king. He had failed Cardoroth. Not that there had ever been much chance that this quest would succeed. They had all known that. But no one, least of all him, had expected it to fail so soon.

He slowed and took some deep breaths. All about him needles rustled, branches moved and the sound of tramping boots filled the shadows. He would be found at any moment, yet whoever did so would regret it. He would take them with him into the great dark. But he knew in his heart that even if he cut a swathe through the enemy, leaving a hill of elug corpses, still more would come. The forest seemed alive with them, and that spelled his death, whether sooner or later.

9. Dust on the Wind

Gilhain surveyed the night.

His view from the tower, looking westward toward Lake Alithorin, was clear. Yet his eyes, though they gazed in that direction and saw whatever could be discerned amid the darkness and shadow, were not really seeing what they looked upon. Or rather, his mind was elsewhere.

In his youth, the land was fair and free. Now, it was surrounded by war. Everything he did, every thought he had, every choice he made was touched by that reality. And he did not like it. No matter that men said he was good at it. No matter that they called him a great strategist and that he preserved the city from destruction. No matter that these things might even be true. He still did not like it.

He would rather the lordships of old where his forefathers had ruled in peace, and their skills were used to improve trade between lands, broker alliances and build the wealth of the nation. And Cardoroth *was* wealthy.

His forefathers had been masters of their skills, each and every bit as much as he was a master of war. But without their actions, he would have no money to provide the soldiers with the best training available. He could not pay them, nor supply them with excellent weapons and armor. Without financial prosperity, his ancestors could not have raised the Cardurleth that protected the city now.

Wealth was the foundation of the city, the basis of the happiness of the people. They did not starve in winter. Their fairs and tournaments were resplendent, their clothes and food and entertainment among the best that he had seen in Alithoras. And he had travelled to many realms in his youth before responsibility weighed him down. He knew it was not so in some cities. He knew that Cardoroth was lucky, though that luck was built on good management. Yet the people, living sheltered lives, did not fully realize how close they were to total destruction. If the enemy prevailed, little would remain of them, or the things they loved.

The name of Cardoroth would endure in memory. The language of the people would still be spoken. Cardoroth, in some way, would survive in the wild lands among far-flung homesteaders and hunters. But those who were not killed in the city would still be cut off from civilization, would soon live a desperate life. They would starve in droughts. Cold would wither the young and frail with sickness and death. Banditry would rise. Knowledge would dwindle, and those folk would regress into the scattered tribes they had once been before the Camar came east, before they learned from the immortal Halathrin. Their past would be black and burned. Their future dim. For they would be hunted too. The enemy would not stop at razing Cardoroth. Its armies would turn to other cities, and would not cease warfare until all Alithoras fell before them. And scattered bands of marauders would linger in each land they conquered and destroyed. The enemy would not leave them to grow again.

There were enemies everywhere, also. Not just outside among elugs and elùgroths. But also inside the city. Lust, greed, abuse of power and the forces of chaos were growing. He had seen the first signs in his youth, and his father had spoken of it often. He did what he could to combat it. But it was a part of humanity and would never be overthrown. As the threat from outside forces grew, so too did it. For some people sought to survive what they thought of as the inevitable fall of the city. It was cursed, the legends said. They called it Red Cardoroth, believing a prophecy that spoke of its utter destruction. And the sorcerers who had been defeated long ago in Queen Carnhaina's time fed it. Their spies and agitators were always at work. And promises of wealth and power came swiftly to their glib tongues.

And if Cardoroth fell, then what next? Faladir? Camarelon? The Free Cities furthest southward that had longest resisted the enemy? The lòhren keep, where the lore and wisdom of Alithoras was preserved, and where lòhrens were trained and then sent out all across the lands as counselors, advisors, healers and resistors of sorcery in order to protect the innocent?

No. None of that could be allowed to come to pass. Cardoroth must survive. It must rebuff the enemy, show that they were not invincible, and help foster resistance among the free peoples of Alithoras. It was his job to ensure that happened, but he needed Brand in order to succeed. He had placed great responsibility on him, but Brand knew all these things as well as he did.

Brand's mind was as sharp as any sword, and his heart was big. He knew how important it all was, and regardless of the fact that most of the nobles of the city called him a wild Duthenor tribesman, he was smarter than they were, more courageous, and had a deeper sense of loyalty. And if the nobles did not like him, Gilhain knew that the general population did. They saw in him an ideal of their own courageous past, for though they dwelled now in prosperity, before their ancestors had founded this realm they had lived a hard life, and the traits to survive that life were important. They were important then, and they were important now, and all the more valued because they were rarer.

But Brand knew little of that. He dealt mostly with the nobility, and they did not hide their attitude. Of the city people he saw little, but Gilhain heard word from trusted servants and gatherers of information what the great majority thought. And they loved him. Gilhain sighed. So did he.

There was movement in the army below, and it recalled Gilhain to his more immediate concerns. What would the enemy do next?

He considered them carefully. They were not just elugs. There were men among their ranks also. The Azan were fierce warriors, and they often marched with elugs. They lived in the same lands far to the south. Usually their elders commanded elug armies, but not this time. This time, the enemy was led by sorcerers; a sign of how committed they were to Cardoroth's destruction.

But elugs, Azan and sorcerers were not the only enemy. There were other dark creatures as well, chief among them the Lethrin.

They were few in number, perhaps only several hundred, but their danger lay in their abilities rather than their numbers.

The Lethrin stood over seven feet, and though Gilhain had never seen them before, rumor carried their tale. They were immensely strong and filled with an implacable hatred of their enemies. Legends said that they were born from the stone of the Graèglin Dennath mountains in the south. Maybe that was so, maybe it was not. But he had seen their skin from a distance during some days when they came to observe battles at the wall, and even from afar he could see that it was tough like hardened leather and would resist the hack and cut of blades. They were miners that hewed tunnels in the rock beneath their mountain homes with massive picks and unwearied arms. Because of their ferocity and overwhelming strength, they usually formed the vanguard of an army, though in this case they were still held in reserve. Over black tunics trimmed with precious stones, they wore silvered chain mail vests that left their arms free. Their mighty hands gripped massive iron maces.

Such were the enemies arrayed against Cardoroth, nor yet had the sorcerers thrown all at them. But that would come. They were slow, but they were relentless. Hatred drove them. And the richness of the north lured them. And there was a shadow behind it all. That much was becoming increasingly clear, Aranloth had warned him. A malevolence controlled things: growing, waxing, nurturing its strength, testing the courage and resilience of the north.

So it had been once before. Ancient enmity lay between north and south, stemming from the time of the exodus when the Halathrin came into Alithoras. They sought to redress a great evil, to defeat it, and so they did, though all of Alithoras was drawn into the Elu-haraken, the Shadowed Wars, of that time. Perhaps that evil was defeated but not destroyed. At least Aranloth hinted that it was so.

Yet even all those were not the only enemies he must counter. His half-brother was somewhere outside Cardoroth, hiding after treachery. He wanted the throne; he had always wanted the throne. He would do anything to get it, and had proven so not that long ago.

Maybe it was not so any longer. The line of the kings had come to an end. A fallen realm needed no king – his brother knew that as well as any.

Gilhain gritted his teeth. His own son had been killed in battle two years ago. When Gilhain died himself, he wanted the crown to pass, assuming the kingdom survived, to his granddaughter. But that was against Cardoroth's traditions. Should he try to force the issue by decree before his death, it might lead to civil war. There would be factions for one side and factions for the other, and his half-brother, much younger, would take advantage of that and assert his claim. But many would never accept him for his past acts of treachery, and his willingness to deal with the enemy.

Gilhain closed his eyes and sighed. The future was bleak, even if the city survived. Unless … unless whoever came after him as king was someone strong, both in a military sense and in the political sense of bringing the people together. His son might have done that, but ill fate had taken him away. There was steel in his granddaughter, but the people of Cardoroth would not be ruled by a woman. Carnhaina was the only ruling queen in their history, yet she was special in many ways, not least of all in having command of a terrible magic.

But his great grandson was a possibility. He was too young of course. He would need a regent, and Gilhain did not trust any save Aranloth or Brand for that job. Any of the nobles would end up assuming the crown in their own name. Yet Aranloth would not be tied down to one place in Alithoras for that long. He would be needed elsewhere. That left Brand, and it was an intriguing thought. He could rule for a time as king, and no other would be better suited, and he trusted him in the end to pass the authority on to his great grandson. Yes, there was an idea there, and though the military commanders would fight it, the ordinary soldiers would all be behind Brand. He had fought with them, spilled blood beside them. Yes, they would be on his side. And that would be enough, assuming Brand was prepared to do it. He had his own problems to solve in his own lands. But ahh! Such thoughts were dust on the wind. It would never happen.

Gilhain started as he saw further movement in the enemy camp. And then the horns began to blow.

Aranloth, standing nearby and looking out, lost in his own thoughts, stood erect. His hands were on the battlements, and they gripped hard until they went white.

"This bodes ill," Gilhain said softly. "There is no attack – not against us. I think they have seen Brand."

Aranloth did not relinquish his fierce grip on the stonework.

"If so, it was not by the vision of mortal eyes, but by sorcery. They guessed our plan, as I thought they would, yet too swiftly. They spend their energy on sorcery now. I can feel it throbbing darkly through the earth and reverberating even in the foundations of the tower on which we stand, but it is not directed at us." He hesitated, thinking with a frown on his face. "The staff gives them powers I do not guess at." He paused again, and he cast down his gaze. "I should not have sent Brand. The powers raised against him, one man alone, are too great. And they will only get worse if he reaches the tombs. I have sent him to his death."

Aranloth bowed his head. The strength left his fingers, and for once he looked what he was: an ancient man who had lived so long that misery, evil, despair and sorrow littered his past, and he could not escape from it.

Gilhain drew a deep breath and steadied his voice against the emotions welling up inside him.

"If he dies," he said, "then we also are dead, and the city and all it protects. And the north is more vulnerable. You're right. It's too much responsibility for one man to bear – too great a trial, and yet, and yet, not for nothing

88

did I make Brand a captain in the army. Not for nothing did I appoint him Durlindrath. He earned those positions by blood and daring when he first came to Cardoroth. I'll not give up until I see a token of his death. If they capture or kill him, the enemy will prove it to us in order to subvert our morale. When they bring forth his corpse, only then will I believe that he is dead."

Aranloth slowly shook his head. "I have seen much death in my long life," he said. "But seldom have I so erred. I should not have sent him, and his blood is on my hands."

"Alas!" Gilhain said. "His death would now be like the death of my son, for so have I come to think of him. But courage, Aranloth! We are two world-weary old men. Brand is young. He is strong. He has luck and courage that I have seldom seen. Let's not second-guess our choices in a moment of doubt. Instead, let's trust our instincts, as he trusts his. A bright day may yet come after the long night."

Aranloth stirred. "May we live to see it."

They spoke no more for some time, lost in their own thoughts once more. But ever their eyes watched the movements of the enemy below. Time passed. Troops moved off into the dark and disappeared from their straining sight. A dim rumor came to them of noise in the distance. Eventually it concentrated, grew louder and clearer, and revealed itself as the rising chant of elùgroths. The sound swelled, and not only were there elùgroths but the fell voices of elugs also.

Aranloth lifted up his head, tilting it as if listening with great care.

Gilhain felt his heart pound. "What new deviltry is this?" he asked. "Will they now attack the wall with sorcery?"

"Nay," Aranloth answered. "This is sorcery, but not what you think. The elùgroths work some new spell. Some summoning, I think. And they augment their power with others. The elugs possess no sorcery, yet the elùgroths are using them in some manner that I have not seen before. But it is not directed at us."

"If it's not directed at us, then—"

"It is for Brand. And may fate grant him mercy."

10. Speak True or Die

Brand took a firm grip on the hilt of his sword.

The enemy was everywhere, and there were perhaps only moments before he was seen. There was no hiding from so many. Nor could he fight them all, though the sword felt light in his hand and his heart raced with anticipation. He would wreak such destruction upon them that they would rue finding him – though they outnumbered him a hundred to one.

Some dark form, tall and lithe, moved from within the concealing shadows of a nearby tree. He prepared to leap and attack, but the soft voice that came out of the dark stilled his feet.

"Come with me – if you want to live."

Brand stood motionless. A dark figure loomed out of the shadows. He saw, revealed now in the dim light, the last thing that he expected. It was a girl, and she was tall and striking. She was clothed in the white robes of a lòhren, yet he saw no staff, but a sword hung at her side.

He hesitated. But the noise of the searchers was loud all around him, and she was no elug. She was as far from that as could be possible. And yet he knew nothing of her, and a mistake now, of any kind, meant death.

He caught the glint of her eyes: anxious, impatient with him and fierce with intelligence. He made up his mind and stepped toward her.

She waited no longer but ducked down beneath a branch and skirted the tree next to her. He followed and found himself racing behind her lithe form along some animal trail that he had not noticed before.

They had gone no further than a few hurried paces when two elugs burst unexpectedly onto the trail from the left. Brand slashed, cutting deep across the throat of the first. It reeled away, but the second shouldered into him, sending him sprawling to the ground and knocking the sword from his hand.

The elug drew its own blade and moved toward him, but Brand whipped out the knife the king had given him and flung it with great force. The gems that formed the sign of bright Halathgar flashed as it flew. It was not a throwing knife, yet it still struck point first, lodging deep in the elug's leather jerkin and sending the creature reeling away. It was not a deathblow, but a bad wound nonetheless.

Brand gathered his sword and stood. The elug staggered away into the dark, the knife still sticking into its body, and Brand made to follow.

The girl had turned and she reached back, grabbing him by the shoulder and pulling him forward.

"We have only seconds!" she whispered. "Let's go!"

Brand knew that she was right, but he felt the loss of the knife as a wrench. It was such a precious gift – gone so soon. Luck and fate were against him this night.

He sheathed his sword and they ran ahead. The trees were dense, and the trail wound through them finding some secret path that no more elugs stumbled onto.

The girl crouched and paused a moment for some reason that he could not tell. Then she stood, tall and still, but seemingly ready to move at the slightest reason. Magic dripped from her fingers as flaming drops, and then she raised both hands and sent flame blasting into a thick stand of bracken.

He could see no reason for her actions, but he had thrown in his lot with hers and must trust to his initial choice.

The foliage was dry, and it erupted in bright fire for several moments, and then thick plumes of smoke billowed from it.

She took his hand and led him into a narrow gully. It was overgrown with more bracken and also many tall ferns. Noise from elugs was all about them. So too was the crackle of flame, but it covered whatever noise they made, and the roiling smoke, spinning, turning and filling the shadowy forest, but especially flowing along the gully, obscured them from view.

They ran ahead for a minute, but then she stopped abruptly again and crouched down. Some way ahead of them a string of elugs crossed the gully, scimitars sweeping through the brush and clearing a way. They pressed on, disappearing into the smoke and shadows, and the girl led Brand forward once more.

They moved faster, for the smoke grew thin and the gully widened. The noise of the elugs was mostly behind them now, somewhere near where the fire had been started.

They moved ahead some more, and then cautiously she led them out of the gully, clambering over some rough ground and then she circled about, heading back to the north and away from the direction Brand wanted to travel, and yet also toward the shore of the lake.

Within several minutes they came to the beach again. She paused there, looking around. She seemed satisfied that the elugs still searched the area of the fire, though it was now fading. Much noise came from there, and it was not that far away, yet there seemed no sign of the enemy just where they were now. Yet still it seemed to him that all she had done was trap them between the water and the forest.

"What now?" he whispered.

She looked at him, and her expression changed. Her hands trembled at her sides, and once more fire dripped from her fingertips.

"Now, you speak the truth or die. You carry Aranloth's staff, and you wear his diadem. Is he dead? Did you have something to do with it? Speak! Or I will blast you to ashes where you stand."

Brand was taken aback by her sudden ferocity, but he held his ground and spoke calmly. This was no time for misunderstandings.

"He gave them to me."

She shook her head and stared at him, if it were possible, even harder.

"That's a lie. You're no lòhren – that much is plain. He would not give you these things. They are precious beyond your understanding."

Brand felt anger surge within him, and his hand found the hilt of his sword.

"Kill me, or try to, if you must. But don't call me a liar."

She considered him. "Kill you I may well yet do. And if I choose so, you will surely perish even as the sun must rise tomorrow. Understand that, and tell me all."

Brand thought hard, and all the while his hand squeezed tightly around his sword hilt. He could not trust anyone with the truth of his quest, least of all a stranger that he had just met. And yet he sensed that her words were not idle. If he tried to deceive her, or tell her less than the truth, one of them would die.

Could he prevail against her? Perhaps. She was confident of her abilities, but she had never met him before and knew nothing of him. He was not easy to kill, magic or no. Yet if she did kill him, and well she might, then Gilhain and Cardoroth were lost.

He looked into her eyes. He read many things there. She was young, but her gaze was that of someone much older. She was a person of great passion, someone who always believed she was right even when she was not. But he also saw concern there. Not for herself; she believed she could kill him easily, but rather for Aranloth. And that was what decided him.

"I told you the truth. Aranloth lent them to me. Why? You had better ask him if you ever get the chance. I don't think they'll do me much good. But he gave them to me for a purpose. That, I will tell you, though once I do, you are at risk of death by not only elugs … but others also, including sorcerers. Think carefully before you insist."

She looked at him sternly. No flicker of doubt crossed her face. All he saw was disbelief – either at all or part of what he said.

"I insist. And don't think that your veiled threat carries any weight. I have little fear of elugs or sorcerers. And less fear of you. Speak!"

Brand told her what he must. He spoke swiftly of the siege of Cardoroth, of an artifact that the elùgroths used to enhance their power. He explained that Aranloth must stay there, with the other lòhrens to hold the enemy off. She seemed doubtful at all this, not convinced that Aranloth would do such a thing, but she did not interrupt.

He told her all that he could, even saying that he must retrieve the second half of Shurilgar's staff, but he did not tell her where he must seek for it.

She listened, but did not lower her hands. "That isn't everything. Tell me all, and then I will decide your fate."

Brand hesitated. Here was a dilemma that none in the city foresaw, not even Aranloth. Yet it was for him to decide now what must be done, and the lòhren and the king could not help. But if he misspoke, then secrets long held could be revealed to the wrong people. Yet there was little in any of it that the enemy did not already guess.

"The second half of the staff has long been hidden in the tombs of the Letharn," he revealed.

At that name a hiss escaped her lips. She stared at him, doubt showing on her face for the first time.

She shook her head. "What could Aranloth possibly be thinking? I don't understand any of this," she said slowly. "You have certainly not revealed all, but you have said enough, at least for the moment. Few know the name that you have just uttered. If nothing else is true, then at least I believe that he told you that. But the staff and the diadem…"

As she spoke she lowered her hands. The fire at her fingertips snuffed out and she straightened.

"Well," she said. "It seems that I must save you after all. But you'll not survive the tombs. That place is dangerous beyond your reckoning, no matter how much Aranloth warned you. The quest will not succeed. You should turn aside from it now, while you still can."

Brand let go of the hilt of his sword, but he did not take his gaze from her.

"I'll not turn aside," he said, suddenly riled. He glared at her for a moment before adding, "And I *will* succeed."

She looked back at him squarely. "So sure?"

"I must be sure," he answered. "Too much depends on it for me to fail, and I will not. Now, what of you? You have magic at your command—"

"Lòhrengai," she interrupted. "The power of lòhrens. Magic is a term which the uneducated use."

Brand gritted his teeth. He had heard the word before, but even Aranloth seemed content for people to say magic.

He shrugged. "Call it what you will. Yet you name yourself a lòhren, and seem keen to prove the point, but where is your own staff? Are you *really* a lòhren? The better now that I see you, and the longer that I talk to you, the more I begin to doubt it."

She looked at him contemptuously. "Maybe I carry no staff just at the moment, but I am, and always will be, a lòhren. Then she added, "My staff was broken."

Brand might be a wild man of the Duthenor, as some in Cardoroth called him, but he knew a lie when he heard it, else he would have died long before he ever came to the city. And that had been a lie. Whether she possessed a staff or not, and whatever might have happened to it he could not know for sure, but he sensed this much at least: it was not broken.

But she need not know that he discerned that. "I must go," he said. "It might still be possible to evade the elugs. You've given me a greater chance at that, so thank you."

He started to move away, truly thankful for what she had done but not wishing to continue their involvement. His instinct was to trust her, but everything she said led him away from that.

"Wait," she said, holding up her palm. "I'll take you away – you won't escape without me. And I'm heading toward the Angle myself, so we may as well journey together, at least part of the way."

Brand looked back at her and showed nothing of what he thought. Yet those words were her second lie. She had not intended until just now to go anywhere near the Angle. And while lòhrens might withhold information, they did not lie.

She might be less than a lòhren, or perhaps in some ways more. But one thing he knew for certain was that she was not what she made herself out to be.

But the question was, what was he going to do about it? He needed help, but dare he trust her?

11. The Gleam of Eyes

Brand had little time to think.

The smoke had dissipated, and the elugs now moved on with their search. He sensed also that there were more of them now. The ones that he had seen so far were just the leaders of the pack – the elùgroths were not taking any chances on his escape.

Before he could do anything there was noise from close by. The two of them hunkered down and remained still. A few moments later several elugs crept through the trees near them, scimitars drawn, but they moved on without pause and soon disappeared into the gloom once more.

Brand waited until he had heard no sound from the group for several minutes before he stood.

The moment of choice was on him, and there would be little time before the next group of elugs came their way. The noise of many nearby told him so.

He gave her a quick nod, signifying that he was willing to join forces, at least for the moment. He would have spoken, but she understood his agreement and lifted a finger to her lips.

She looked around, perhaps using senses other than sight to locate the elugs, and then she leaned in close and whispered softly in his ear.

"They are all around us," she said. "They fill the forest, but they cannot search the lake. Stay silent. Watch. And learn."

She stepped back from him, leaning against a tree trunk and almost disappearing even from his own view.

And though he could barely see her, he could hear her. She muttered under her breath. He could not catch the words, nor even the language, for her voice was so soft as to seem little more than the faint rustle of leaves or the slow creak of branch and root in the forest.

She was not speaking to him. Rather, she softly chanted into the night, for though he understood nothing of what she said, he heard the rhythmic rise and fall of her voice. What she was doing he did not know, except that it was some kind of magic – or lòhrengai as she would have him call it.

He looked about him in the dark. He saw nothing happening, but then again he did not know what to look for. Whatever else she was, she had power at her command, and she was invoking it now for a purpose. He must watch and wait to see what it was.

Harsh voices drifted through the forest. The elugs called to one another. Perhaps they had seen some mark or track of those they pursued. The night grew darker. Everything seemed breathless, and the pinewoods brooded in shadowy stillness.

He looked away from the forest and out over the beach, and then to the lake. The first tendrils of fog were rising from it. He nearly looked away again, but then he realized something was wrong.

The silvery tendrils moved ahead and rose up onto the beach with purpose, probing their way toward the tree line. He had seen fog like that before, and recently. It reminded him of the sorcerous attack on the king.

Even as he watched the fog gathered speed. It grew thicker too, rising now in clouds above the lake like steam from boiling water.

Long vaporish arms reached out, stretched into the trees and caused things to become even darker. It sailed above their heads, blotting out the starlight. Soon it was so thick that very little could be seen at all.

It was cold and clammy. But then he felt her hand, surprisingly warm against his own, and she led him away from their hiding spot and down through the thick fog onto the beach. No one could see them now, but the water would be dangerously cold and he saw no real hope of escaping that way.

She led him over the rough sand. They were nothing more than two fleeting half-shadows in a world of mist, and for the first time in a while he felt safe. Yet with that thought came the realization that fog or not, there were very many eyes that sought him. Safety was scarcer at the moment than light itself.

The rough sand gave way to a muddy surface. The actual water's edge was still a little way off, but guiding him firmly with her hand the girl did not lead him to it but parallel with it. That puzzled him.

Reeds grew about them. They rustled as the two of them entered, and the noise grew louder but it could not be helped. The reeds swiftly grew tall and thick, but go as slow as she might yet still every movement sent a shiver up their stalks and shook down cold drops of water.

He knew it would be hard to spot in the murk, but they had left a trail over the sand and into the reeds. It would not be hard to follow once seen, and he did not like it. Still less did he like not knowing what her plan was. Yet she had one, of that he was certain.

She paused, becoming suddenly still. He stood behind her, barely daring to breathe, but he heard nothing. Nor could he see anything, for the reeds and fog obscured all. There was only her firm handgrip: warm, strong, confident.

He realized that it was not just quiet. It was *too* quiet. There was no sound among the trees of searching elugs, either close at hand or far away. There was no noise of shouts and harsh voices. There was nothing save the whisper of wet reeds close by and a brooding menace from the dark of the trees further away, which he could not see but still felt.

"There's something wrong," she whispered. "The enemy is close, for all their silence, but it's as if they're waiting. For what, I cannot guess."

Brand knew she was right, and he had no desire to *try* to guess. Whatever reason they had, it was unlikely to mean anything good.

She sensed his mood and began to move again, drawing him forward more swiftly now, almost careless of noise.

The reeds gave way at length, and they stood in a kind of clearing. Wet sand and gravel churned beneath their feet, but the reeds were still all around. It was like a little glade in the forest. But the reeds now seemed ominous rather than their friend. While they were in them, they offered cover. In the open, surrounded by them, they were a place where their enemies could hide – could be hiding even now, peering through stems and fog to study their prey.

She moved to the left. The shore was there, the silvery water of the lake still and placid. She stepped into the water.

Brand wondered if he should discard his chain mail. He was loath to do so, for it might yet save his life, but it might also kill him in the water.

But she did not lead him in any deeper than a foot or so. She moved back into the reeds, though he saw these were now of a different kind: taller, thinner, more grass-like.

Within moments she found what she sought, and he better understood her plan.

"I didn't know you had a boat," he whispered.

"It's a shuffa," she corrected. "At least, that's what my people used to call them."

She took hold of the craft and deftly undid the rope that held it to the base of some bunched reeds. The vessel was strange to Brand's eyes, nearly round, and made of some light timber over which was stretched hide. It hardly looked like it would serve as a boat, but he did not question her. That, he guessed, would prove fruitless.

"Are you any good with boats?" she asked.

Brand shook his head. His people were farmers rather than fishermen. He'd had little experience of such things, and as usual, she had a knack for pinpointing his weaknesses.

"Never mind," she answered shortly. "I'll take us out into the water. Step carefully, and don't turn us over as you move around."

She took the only oar in the shuffa and steadied herself with it while she stepped in and gracefully sat down.

Brand gritted his teeth and followed suit. He moved carefully, yet still the boat wobbled dangerously in the water.

The girl stared at him, but held her tongue until he was seated.

"Ready?" she asked.

But then she began to row without waiting for his response. With slow but powerful strokes she got them underway. She took great care to paddle smoothly so that there was barely any noise and no splashing of water.

The shuffa moved into deeper water. It floated very well, surprisingly well to Brand considering it was little more than a near round shell, but it was hard to steer. At times she rowed with her back to the shore, at others the craft spun around in the water and she rowed facing it. Yet slowly and surely they drew away from the bank.

The land was now a vague line. The beach stood out, a pale strip in the fog, and the forest beyond was nothing more than a dark smudge. But from that smudge elugs suddenly emerged. They paused, saw their prey, and then drew their bows to shoot. It was some distance, yet not so far that arrows could not kill, though the accurate aiming of them would be harder.

Brand hunkered down, lifting up Aranloth's staff and lowering his head so that his helm would better protect him.

The girl paddled faster now, careless of the noise. Secrecy and quiet no longer served.

Arrows whistled past in the dark. Some struck the water nearby. Some flew wild into the fog. One would have struck him as the boat tilted sideways but with a deft movement and surprising reflexes the girl flicked the oar and deflected it.

After that, the arrows began to fall short or go wide. They were now very nearly out of sight, and deep within the fog that still rose from the cold waters of the lake.

The elugs stopped shooting. Not only that, their dim forms seemed to part: some moving left and others right. Brand thought it strange, for they might yet have continued to shoot a few moments longer.

The girl slowed her rowing a little. "Once again I've saved your life. Am I going to have to baby you all the way to the Angle?"

Brand felt his patience slip. Yet what she said was true. She *had* saved his life several times tonight. He owed her, and he did not take such debts lightly. Yet it was irksome, for it meant that she held power over him. Despite her manner, there was something about her that attracted him also: she was dangerous, strong willed, beautiful and mysterious. He wanted to see her in the light of day, and that line of thought upset him. It was another way that she might hold power over him, and he did not like that. He did not like it at all

He looked back at the barely visible shore, and thought that they were free. But it was not so. Through the parted ranks of the elugs he saw a shadow. Swift it came onward, and the elugs recoiled further away from it. And then he realized that it was not one shadow, but three.

Whatever they were, they leapt out from the shore as one, and though they made no sound of themselves, their huge bodies crashed into the water with a great splash. Foamy water frothed all around them and great waves spread out.

The girl rowed faster. Brand studied the creatures, but he could not tell what they were, except that they were not elugs. They were something else entirely.

As he watched they continued to swim, pressing closer. He saw that they were four legged, for they had the form of massive hounds, yet they held their heads high up out of the water, and there was a look to them that was not as of a hound, but rather of an elug – or a man.

A chill ran up Brand's spine. Foul sorcery! For whatever these creatures were, they did not swim or tread the earth of their own volition. They were made, called forth as were the drùghoth, and he sensed in the growing gleam of their approaching eyes a desperate madness.

The foul beasts drew closer. The elugs, closing ranks again, began to hoot and shout.

They faded from view, but the beasts came on faster than the girl could row. Or else they still ran, their great paws reaching down to the lake bottom, for he saw that they were massive, much larger than any wolf or hound that he had ever seen.

He cast about desperately for something to do to help the girl, but he had no bow, and there was only one paddle, and she was more skilled with it than he.

The shuffa came to deeper water. The fog thickened, but the beasts were closer, and he saw malevolence in their blood-shot eyes. And he felt the ill will of the sorcerers who had created them, looking out and staring at him hungrily.

12. We Do Not Yield!

Gilhain was surrounded by the Durlin. He trusted them. They called him by name, and he knew as much, or perhaps more, of their everyday lives as their friends did. Yet without Brand among them, at one moment solemn and deadly serious, at another laughing and carefree, but ever-watchful, he felt suddenly vulnerable.

The Durlin had courage, but when necessity demanded, pure ice ran through Brand's veins. He knew fear, as any wise man did, but it never stopped him. Where other men hesitated, he acted. Where other men were cowed by terror, he stood tall. Where other men broke, he found strength within himself to endure. He had proven all these things, or Gilhain would not have made him Durlindrath.

Without his constant shadow, ever-present but always in the background, Gilhain realized how easy it would be for an assassin to kill him. The Durlin were good, the best bodyguards in all of Alithoras, but without Brand to lead them they were lessened. For it was not skill that made the difference, nor friendship, but a deep and abiding affection more like that between father and son.

Gilhain shrugged his worries aside. He could not function if he dwelled on the risk to himself, and Cardoroth *needed* him to function. The attacks of the enemy had stepped up. It was the next day after Brand had left, and something had stiffened the enemy's resolve. All night their sorcerous chanting rolled and echoed through the city. At dawn, the attacks began. Wave after wave of maddened elugs sought to take the walls. Aranloth claimed the elùgroths used sorcery to work them into a frenzy, and Gilhain believed it.

Another attack was forming now. The war drums beat louder than ever. The elug chant, not sorcerous as was that of the elùgroths, yet still a powerful sap to morale, rose and beat at the Cardurleth like a physical assault:

Ashrak ghùl skar! Skee ghùl ashrak!
Skee ghùl ashrak! Ashrak ghùl skar!

The chant ran without beginning or end. The drums became one with it, or it one with the drums. The elugs stamped their iron-shod boots. Terror rose like a dust cloud, choking the air and making it hard to breathe. All along the walls men stood still, heads down, ashen-faced and scared. That chant had signaled the fall of many cities before now, and they wondered if it was their turn. Everyone knew what the words meant:

Death and destruction! Blood and death!
Blood and death! Death and destruction!

But Gilhain was no longer prepared to let the chant go unchallenged. If the will of the defenders was sapped before the fighting began, the wall might well fall. And the attack that was building was a great one. He felt that in his bones. People called him a strategist. That might be so, but most of his strategy was simple. Attack when he had an advantage. Defend when he was disadvantaged. And never allow the enemy to have everything their own way.

He stepped forward and gestured to his standard-bearer. The man lifted up high the flag that all the kings of Cardoroth had used: a sable background threaded with a gold eagle, one taloned claw lifted and raking at an invisible enemy, the wings half stretched out.

At the same moment a blast from one of the great Carnyx horns, a relic of the ancient Camar past, sounded. It was a challenge in itself to the enemy chant. But Gilhain added to it when its long notes finally died away. His deep voice rolled far along the walls, carrying to many of his men and also the front ranks of the enemy:

> *Death and destruction. Blood and death.*
> *Red shall elugs bleed! Swift shall elugs die!*

His men lifted their heads. Some laughed. Some gripped their swords tightly and raised their heads to stare angrily at the enemy. Some repeated the cry until it was taken up by many and rolled from the walls to smash against the chant of the elugs like two great waves crashing against each other.

The elugs stamped their boots faster. A horn sounded from somewhere amid their host and the front ranks of the enemy broke away from the vast mass behind it. The charge toward the wall had begun.

The men on the wall were ready for it. Gilhain watched from the west tower. Aranloth stood beside him.

"That was well done," the lòhren said.

Gilhain shrugged. "A small thing, but effective."

"A small thing, you say. But useless if done at the wrong moment. You didn't invent your twist on the chant just then. It's been on your mind for days, perhaps even weeks. You waited until now to use it, on the day when the enemy bends their will most strongly upon our destruction."

Gilhain shrugged again, but this time a smile flickered across his face before he answered.

"But the real point is this – why do they bend their will on our destruction? I mean, why today more than any other?"

The lòhren cast his gaze out over the wall at the charging enemy. "I don't know, but it's so. That much we can both feel."

There was no more time for talk. The great mass of the enemy drew near the Cardurleth. The sound of so many tramping boots, of wild yells and the incessant pounding of drums from within the main host rose in a menacing din that seemed to shake the very stone of the wall. But those who held it did not flinch.

The men hefted spears, drew bows and grasped rocks. The arrows sped forth first, swift-flighted darts that hissed through the air and struck death from afar. The elugs wore armor, though many only had leather jerkins. The great bows of Cardoroth were strong, and hardened leather offered little protection even from a distance. Many fell, tripping and hindering their fellows. But the mad rush continued and none slowed, for to slow was to become a target for the bowmen.

On the dark ranks raced. Arrows sang among them, but now also the spears were hurled. They were heavy, and sharp tipped, and they rained a deadly hail upon the enemy. Yet still the elugs came, trampling over their dead or wounded, screaming in rage or fear and especially for the sheer madness that the elùgroths had instilled in them during the night by sorcerous chanting.

The rocks came next. Some were thrown like balls. Others, so large that two men had to heave them, dropped over the wall. Just as the elugs reached the Cardurleth this latest defense assaulted them, but they had reached some measure of safety now, being so close to the wall where arrows and spears were of less use.

The elugs threw up the ladders they carried. They were rickety constructions of light timber, held together by twine and hope. But they also had climbing ropes with steel barbed hooks at the end. All were thrown against the wall. And the enemy that yet lived, which was still the greater part of them, commenced to climb.

The men of Cardoroth worked speedily now, but with calm and efficiency. Gilhain gave no orders, nor did the captains along the wall. The soldiers knew what needed doing, and when, and they acted accordingly.

They used long poles to dislodge the ladders, sending the elugs screaming to death or broken bones below. Axes cut at ropes, though some of these were wound with wire also and that slowed their severing. Yet hundreds of the enemy hurtled to grim deaths, for it was a long climb.

Yet climb the enemy did, swarming up the wall until the forerunners clambered through some of the gaps at the top of the crenellated battlement.

The elugs slipped through, or jumped or leaped or rolled, but they came to their feet and wielded their curved blades with ferocity and desperation. For though they had attained the battlement, the greatest risk was now upon them. Many were cut and stabbed by sword as they reached the top. Those who survived this deadly greeting were few, and the mass of men atop the battlement pressed against them with grim determination.

But the elugs fought on. A trickle of their fellows joined them. There were now more elugs atop the wall than there had ever been before, and the enemy took hope from this. If they could but hold on a little while until more of their kind came, the wall might yet fall. And should that happen the city would swiftly follow.

The elugs fought with crazed desperation. The men hacked and slew with quiet determination. Blood slicked the stone. Screams rang out. The stench of death hung heavy over the walls. In the distance crows flapped on their perches in tall trees, croaking and sharpening their beaks. High overhead the Red Kites of Cardoroth, which lived off vermin and refuse, circled the airs.

In the enemy camp the war drums rose in sudden frenzy, and the whole host beat swords on shields and stamped their iron-shod boots. The din was maddening, and fear throbbed through the air.

Gilhain stepped forward and gave a signal. His standard-bearer lifted high his flag and the great carnyx horn sounded again. For just a moment every eye that could turned toward him.

The king drew his sword. It was the sword of his father, and his father's father. It leaped like a white flame from its sheath, but bright red sparks shimmered from its gem-encrusted pommel.

"The Cardurleth has never fallen," he cried. "Nor will it! Not while brave men hold its length. And you are as brave as any that defended the city during our long history. Teach these elugs what all their kind before them have learned: we do not yield!"

The men drove against the elugs with all their might. The elugs fought back, panic lending them ferocity, for should they fail to take the wall every one of them was dead.

For several long breaths Gilhain watched. He could not tell who would prevail, and he was ready to step forth and fight himself, for that would hearten the defenders. Yet if he did that now it would have less effect at some time in the future when the defenders might need it more.

He waited. Men died. Elugs died. The battlements roiled with the finely balanced potentials of victory and defeat.

Gilhain glanced at Aranloth. The lòhren stood, transfixed by the battle, his hands gripping his oaken staff, his eyes seeming to follow every slash and cut of a thousand blades. But he gave no sign of what he thought.

The decision was Gilhain's. He moved his right foot, preparing to step forward, but instinct told him to wait, and he listened to it.

The elugs pressed forward. They took the battlement inch by inch, but they did so in only a few places. In others, the men of Cardoroth held their own. New elugs scrambled up the ladders and climbing ropes, but many of these devices had been cut or destroyed the first time they were dislodged. There were much less now, and the newcomers were therefore fewer, and within a minute the men of Cardoroth pressed back. Soon no new elugs reached the battlement, for there was no way for them to pass through the ranks of their brethren, pushed right back against the stonework.

The men of Cardoroth were tired. Their sword strokes were slower, less powerful, and the elugs fought with the knowledge that this might be their last few moments walking in the world.

But the men outnumbered them, and though slowed by exhaustion, determination kept them on their feet. They continued to press their enemy, and in moments the tide turned. The elugs knew they had now lost and the fight went out of them. Resigned to death, they fell swiftly, their dark bodies littering the stone floor of the battlement, those that were not lifted and cast over the wall.

113

The last elug fell. A hush descended. The war drums came to a rumbling stop.

"We survive yet again," whispered Gilhain.

Aranloth let out a sigh beside him. "So it seems, though that was closer than I would have liked." His keen-eyed glance fell upon Gilhain. "You have nerves of ice. Few others in your position would have waited so long. But your own blade will yet be needed. Whether today, or tomorrow, or in a month. Keep it sharp!"

Gilhain grunted. "The blade is sharp, but the arm that wields it has lost its strength of old."

'Maybe so, but the mind that guides it is still strong and sure."

Gilhain watched as the men went to work. They moved quickly, for no one knew how long it would take for the next assault to come. But for the moment, the enemy remained subdued, and no sign of a further attack seemed imminent.

The wounded were removed first, taken below into the city to the care of the healers. Not that all of them would live. Many might though, and still have productive lives though maimed in body and mind. The dead were removed next. Elugs were tumbled over the wall, the men of Cardoroth taken away with solemnity. Then came the buckets of water to wash away the gore, and swiftly after that sawdust to soak up any moisture. The battlement was no place for a slippery surface where men could fall.

Gilhain kept his gaze on the enemy. He wanted to read what they would do next, for most of what he did as commander relied on discerning the intentions of the enemy. Yet he was perplexed at the moment. The opposing host had suffered a defeat, perhaps a great one, for they had worked themselves into a frenzy all night in order to try to win the fight today. They had lost, and yet now was also the time to attack. The defenders on the wall were weary. Their spirits might be high, but if the enemy could not take the walls in a single assault they must show that they had the numbers to keep on coming back, even after a defeat. That would be the most demoralizing message of all, and yet no attack came.

"What are they doing?" Gilhain asked the lòhren.

Aranloth followed his gaze. "The unexpected," he said.

"What do you mean?"

"Look to the center of the host. There is movement there."

Gilhain did so. "All I can see are a few figures coming forward. It's not an attack."

"Not of arms," Aranloth answered.

"Then what? Sorcery? I see now that the figures are black-cloaked elùgroths."

"Perhaps," Aranloth said slowly. "I don't rule that out, but I think this is something else. We shall see soon."

They watched as the figures came to the front of the host. There were three elùgroths and three men of the Azan race.

The elùgroths clutched their wych-wood staffs, and the Azan stood meekly behind them. Yet what the purpose of the enemy was, no one knew.

The men on the walls watched keenly, and Gilhain kept an eye on the soldiers' reaction also, for so far the sorcerers had stayed back and let the elugs attack. The men were familiar with the chanting at night, the words of power that rolled through the enemy host intended to uplift the dark horde and at the same time weaken the determination of the defenders. They knew that a sorcerous attempt had been made on his life, but they must wonder even as did he, what would be next?

115

But of that, Gilhain could not even guess, and it disturbed him. Whatever it was, as Aranloth had said, it would be unexpected.

13. A Token of Death

Gilhain watched nervously, but he did not allow any of his inner feelings to show. He stood casually, his hands clasped behind his back, as if he surveyed nothing more than the scenery on a morning walk.

The elùgroths left the ranks of the host and came forward. Their strides were long and confident. The one in the middle held his wych-wood staff loosely in his left hand. Something small caught the sun in his right.

Gilhain stepped to the edge of the wall and leaned against it. Aranloth followed.

"What do they want?" Gilhain asked.

"They do not want anything. They come to tell us something, and it will not be good. Prepare yourself."

Gilhain did not move, but his heart sunk and his stomach churned.

The elùgroths drew closer, the three Azan that served them following close behind.

"The one in the middle is Khamdar," Aranloth said. "He is the leader of the elùgroths gathered here."

Gilhain studied him. He was very tall, and he strode with confidence, or perhaps arrogance. He showed no doubt and no fear at approaching the wall so closely. Gilhain considered ordering a hail of arrows, but that was not just, for these men had come to parley, however evil they were. More than that, he doubted they were vulnerable to arrow attack, or else they would not venture so close in the first place, and seeing such an attack fail would dishearten the men and rally the elugs. He waited, unmoving and patient.

The elùgroths came beneath the shadow of the wall, and there they stopped.

"Be wary," Aranloth hissed. "Khamdar is dangerous. Everywhere he goes he leaves death and woe behind him as other men leave trails in the snow."

Gilhain did not answer. There was nothing he could say.

In the shadow of the Cardurleth the sorcerers stirred. Khamdar muttered something to those beside him, and then he looked up.

Even from the ground below, Gilhain felt the force of his stare. The man's head was cowled, which shadowed his face, and though no eyes were visible, yet still Gilhain sensed their probing. And it was more than probing; it was a wave of malice that smote the wall and those upon it as a physical blow.

Some of the men took a step back. Some gripped their swords in trembling hands. Gilhain stood still and waited.

Khamdar raised his wych-wood staff. The dark wood was dull in the shadows, but the long-fingered hand that held it, pallid and blue-veined, was clearly visible. Gilhain reminded himself that the sorcerer was a man, whatever his age or powers – however he looked and acted. He was still a man.

"I come not to offer hope," Khamdar said.

His voice was slow and deep. It welled up to the battlement like a rising tide, and by some art of sorcery it carried far along the wall to either side.

"I come to take it away. Today, there will be no granting of mercy. We will not promise to let you live if you surrender. We will not depart, though you try to buy freedom with a hundred wagons laden with heavy gold."

Gilhain finally moved. He gave a nonchalant shrug.

"Tell us something new," he said, and by the power of Aranloth his words were also carried far across the wall and even to the enemy host.

"Since when do elug armies grant mercy? Since when did elùgroths become noble leaders? Try to kill us with blades or sorcery if you must, but don't be so stupid as to think that words will purchase what only blood and courage can buy."

There was a sharp hiss from one of the Azan men below, but the elùgroths showed no reaction.

Khamdar laughed into the sudden silence. It was a fell sound, like a wolf's howl born on a midnight wind, and Gilhain's blood ran cold. He wondered if his enemy was a man after all.

"So brave!" Khamdar cried. "Well, bravery is for those who possess hope. But the hopeless fall away and die. You shall see that my words are true, but first I would speak with the old man beside you. To him would I bring tidings of events beyond this wall."

Aranloth did not move, but his voice rang out.

"Speak then, Khamdar, lòhren that was. But we shall judge the truth of your words."

"Truth?" Khamdar answered. "You do not recognize truth when you see it. Through the ages you have blindly fought the long defeat. For there is no stopping my kind, or the power that we serve. Still, you try. And that is a noble, if foolish, thing. Yet nobler would it have been for you to die in one of the many battles that you have seen. But no, you endure while others fight and die, giving their lives for your cause. Is that not so?"

Aranloth remained still. "It is not, but speak on. I do not have all day to exchange insults with a renegade that deserted his friends. But tell me this – was it worth it? You betrayed the lòhrens in search of power. Have you found it? Or have you found only servitude instead?"

Khamdar snarled. "Betrayed! It was you who held me back!"

A wave of malice drove against the wall, and the anger in the sorcerer's voice throbbed through the air.

Khamdar was silent a moment, as though gathering scattered thoughts that he had lost.

"Ever you know how to use words to twist things," he said at length. "Was it not so with Brand?"

He paused, and Gilhain leaned closer against the wall.

"Ah," the elùgroth said, looking at him. "I see that the name is not unknown to you. Nor to me. For I have met Brand."

Khamdar turned to Aranloth again.

"Would you like to know, O mighty lòhren, what his last words were?"

Aranloth gripped tight his staff.

"You will speak, whether I will or no, so get to it."

"Very well. I have no wish to prolong your pain. I will tell you, but first, I think that perhaps all the men who so valiantly protect both king and lòhren should know what the last hope of Cardoroth was, how the city leaders devised it, and who they sent in their stead for its accomplishment. Who, in fact, faced dangers beyond them so that cowards might live a little while longer."

A hush fell over the wall, and Khamdar paused. His words were dripping with poison. They could fester among the men, and Gilhain knew he should say something. But he was overwhelmed. The enemy knew of Brand. They said he was dead, and that wrenched at him even more than he feared it would, but he straightened and took heart. Words were often easy to say – proof was harder.

Khamdar spoke again. His voice was slow and assured.

"We elùgroths possess great power," he said. "But there is an object that we use to enhance it. Your leaders," and here he pointed at Gilhain and Aranloth with his staff, "sought to break that power. They sent Brand, your precious Durlindrath, on a quest to do so. They sent him alone. One man against an army. That was so ... *brave* ... of them, was it not? But Brand is now dead, though he lived a long time, despite torture and torment. Yet with his dying breath he cursed both lòhren and king."

He turned again to Aranloth.

"Does that surprise you? It should not. You sent someone to complete a task that you dared not attempt yourself, and he died in your stead. What else did you expect?"

Aranloth gave no answer, but he leaned on his staff and bowed his head.

Gilhain spoke. "You have much to say, but I see no evidence that your words are anything more than dust on the wind."

Khamdar laughed again. "Dust on the wind? Then let the air bring you the proof you want!"

He drew back his arm, and though the wall was high, and Gilhain stood more than fifty feet above him, the elùgroth hurled an object with speed and accuracy. It flashed through the air, spinning and glittering as it wheeled.

It would have struck Gilhain even though he tried to leap back, but Aranloth was quicker than he looked, or perhaps had anticipated such a move. Either way, his staff struck the object down to clatter on the stone flagging at their feet. The lòhren bent down quickly to pick it up.

From the ramparts several archers loosed arrows. But no shaft reached the target below. With a dismissive wave of the wych-wood staff the arrows shattered in flight and fell whining in smoke and ruin.

"Halt!" cried Gilhain, holding up his hand to stop any further attack. "Don't fire."

The men fitted new arrows to their strings, but did not draw.

"This is a parley," Gilhain said, moving back to the edge of the wall. "But I suppose I shouldn't expect elùgroths to hold to the rules of civilization."

Khamdar looked up at him and grinned. The cowl fell back a little and there was a sudden flash of white teeth and also a high-cheeked but pale face.

"It was no attack – merely a returning of your own. But think on how I came to possess it? See! Aranloth already knows."

Gilhain turned to the lòhren. Aranloth stood there, his head bowed and his posture limp. Yet in one hand he held a knife, the very knife that Gilhain had given the previous night to Brand. He knew it by the sign of Halathgar that was on it. It had not brought Brand the luck he needed…

The elùgroth spoke again. His voice was cold.

"We know your purpose. We learned your plans. Your hope is lost, and the city will fall. The proof is in the lòhren's own hand."

The elùgroth turned on his heel and strode back toward the camp. It was a dismissive gesture, but one that his comrades did not imitate. They backed away carefully, keeping a close eye on the ramparts for any further arrow shot, but it was needless. Gilhain's command held firm, and the men did not draw their bows.

The lòhren staggered back from the rim of the wall. He looked as ancient as he was, and Gilhain's own heart

122

sank in anguish. Their last hope was truly lost, and Brand, like a son to him, was gone with it.

The retreating elùgroths merged back into the host. Aranloth stood there, leaning on his staff as though it were all that held him upright.

"We tried," Gilhain said. "But Cardoroth will fall, sooner or later. And Brand will neither walk its streets nor return to the lands of the Duthenor. I wish now that we had not sent him."

Aranloth slowly straightened. He lifted up his head, and though his face did not alter, Gilhain saw that some great emotion flowed through him like a river, and the power that he veiled ran near the surface. Then it was gone, and the lòhren went back to normal, but he laughed and a look of merriness was in his eyes.

Gilhain stepped back another pace, but the lòhren raised a hand and stayed him.

"O king! Do not think I am mad. Grief has not broken me, though well it might have through the long years. If I seem other than you expect, it is because the situation is not what it seems. Khamdar is a *liar*. Thus he has ever been, but this is the happiest lie ever he told. Brand is not dead."

Gilhain looked at him. Then he looked at what the lòhren held in his hand.

"But he has given us the proof of his words. The knife is the token of death that we feared."

Aranloth shook his head. "No. It is not. You do not know Khamdar as I do. I said he was evil, and evil shows us what it is by its nature. If he had taken Brand, he first would have learned what he could from him, and then, in order to weaken us, he would have had him tortured and slain before the walls. And if Brand were killed when they tried to capture him, then Khamdar would have brought and then broken his body before us. That is his nature, to inflict pain, both physical and emotional. You can be sure that Brand yet lives, and somewhere out there," the lòhren gestured widely with the knife in his hand, "he still strives to fulfill the quest."

Gilhain slowly reached out and took the knife. He studied it carefully. There was no doubt that it was the very same that he had given Brand. Yet it was a thing of luck, and suddenly, despite what the elùgroth would have him believe, he saw many ways that it might come into the possession of the enemy, and yet by luck Brand might have escaped their grasp.

He felt hope surge through his veins once more and looked up. Tears misted his vision and he felt ten years younger. Joy surged within him just as it had a few moments ago in the lòhren.

"But why then this act? Why pretend to believe the elùgroth?"

Aranloth grinned. "Let them think we are beaten. The soldiers on the wall know little of Brand or his quest. They trust rather to their own strength of arms. Let that continue. In the meantime, if the enemy thinks you broken, they will be less swift to try to kill you. That is to our advantage. Never let the enemy know what you are really thinking. You know that."

Gilhain grinned back at him.

"So I do. We'll turn this to our benefit, and I'll make them rue the day they tried to break me."

Aranloth sighed, and as swiftly as joy had shone from his face, it now faded.

"Alas, joy is always short lived. Brand yet lives, but I do not doubt that they know of him, that they have learned his purpose and hunt him. He is not dead, at least not yet, but neither will he know safety again for a long while."

Gilhain understood the truth of those words. And yet having felt despair only moments before, he would not allow it to overwhelm him again, no matter what the enemy said or did, no matter that hope was as tenuous as a fluttering heartbeat.

14. Forbidden Lore

Brand drew his sword. The hounds swam toward the little boat. For all their splashing and the froth of water about them, they came on in unnatural silence. But still they came on.

The girl rowed as swiftly as she could, but the shuffa was not a fast vessel. She would never outpace them.

Brand stood up, carefully keeping his balance by spreading his legs. He could not fight properly like this, but it was all he could do.

The shuffa began to spin to the side, taking him away from facing their enemy. The girl tried to right the boat, but all she could manage for the moment was keeping it at the same angle, yet still they drew away from the bank. It was now invisible, swathed in the thick fog.

For the first time one of the hounds made a noise. It was a deep howl, like that of a wolf's, but Brand heard words weaved through it, and it held something of the timbre of a human voice.

The other two hounds took up the howl, and the girl began to slow her rowing. In a moment, Brand saw why.

The craft was now in deeper water, and the hounds seemed to have come as far as they dared. They were not good swimmers, being heavy set, and their thick wet fur weighed them down. Great tufts stood out in places, while in others only pale skin showed.

The howling ended in vicious snarls, and the beasts turned back toward the shore. The girl did not stop rowing.

In the following moments they ventured further out into the lake. Shore and elugs and hounds were gone. He was alone with the girl in a world of water and thick fog.

It was eerily quiet, and she was obviously unsettled. Whatever the beasts were, they were not natural. They were a product of sorcery, and he thought it must be a great sorcery at that. But it did not bear thinking about too deeply, for however it was done he guessed that not just beasts were involved, but also men. In some manner the elùgroths had fused both together, and it was an abomination such as only they could conceive. He remembered Aranloth's words that even among elùgroths, Khamdar was the worst. If he did not believe it before, he did now.

The girl turned the boat southward. How she knew which direction was which, he did not know. But she told him so and he believed her.

They took turns at rowing. He found it cumbersome, but soon grew competent after her terse instructions. It was not that difficult, but neither was their rate of progress fast. Still, the enemy could not see or track them, and so far as he knew, they could not discover in what direction his quest lay. Only Aranloth and Gilhain knew that, and in them he trusted.

Only the distant sounds from shore kept them from straying too far out over the lake. He could not tell himself in which direction they were headed, but at least he knew they were not getting lost on the vast expanse of water. At first they heard elugs, but when the noise of their tramping through the brush and calls to one another faded, there was only the occasional hoot of an owl or yelp of a fox.

When the silvery dawn finally glimmered through the fog, they could dimly see the shore again and struck out toward it. As the light grew, Brand could see his companion better. Her eyes were green with flecks of brown. Or else they were brown with flecks of green. He could not tell which. And what he had taken for white lòhren robes were not. Rather, she wore a flowing tunic, all of pale gray and tied at her waist with a black belt.

He studied her closely now, for suspicion rose in him, and a terrible fear that he had made the most dreadful mistake – notwithstanding that he had not had any choice.

Her hair was long and ash-blonde, bound by a black ribbon. She gazed back at him with eyes that sparkled not just with intelligence but also secrets. But for all her fierce gaze she was even more beautiful than he had thought, though it was beauty of a high and remote kind.

With an insight that surprised him, he realized that few people ever got close enough to her to discover what she really thought or felt. She held everyone at a distance, even as she was doing with him.

She grew annoyed at his scrutiny, but before she could say anything he spoke.

"Are you not lonely? You know, independence is a fine thing, but sometimes it's nice to be able to lean on others when you most need it."

She gazed at him with such fierceness that he thought she was going to attack him, and Aranloth's diadem felt hot against the skin of his forehead.

"What business is it of yours?" she snapped.

"Oh, I know a thing or two of loneliness. I'm a Duthenor tribesman, the only of my kind in a great city with a recorded history stretching back into what my people think of as legend. My family is dead. And they did not die of old age. And what was theirs was stolen from them. Yes, I know a thing or two of loneliness. But if you're content so, then there is no need to speak of it."

128

"I'm content," she said, but for a moment it seemed to him that she drew a veil over her face, and yet he glimpsed a little of what lay behind it. And a flicker in her eyes gave the lie to her words, for he momentarily saw a yearning in them every bit as fierce as her independence.

He let the matter drop. They were getting close to the shore now, and he trained his attention on it.

"The enemy could be out there," he said. "We wouldn't know if they were swarming beyond the beach and in the trees."

The girl shrugged with nonchalance, as though what he said did not matter, or was wrong.

"Maybe," she replied. "But they can't know where we'll make land. Lake Alithorin is vast, and I'm pretty happy with our chances of avoiding them – at least for now."

"If they're not here, and I agree with you for the moment, they'll sooner or later find our tracks wherever we come to shore, and follow."

"That's a given," she said, flicking her hair impatiently. "And don't forget those beasts. I guess they'll have your scent, and the water won't put them off forever." She paused, and stared straight at him. "Are you scared? Do you wish to abandon your quest so soon, even though I'm babying you through it?"

That made him angry. She seemed one of the few people able to draw that emotion out of him with ease.

"You've helped me," he said with deliberate slowness, "and I thank you for it. But I don't take the names of scared or baby from anyone. Not from a warrior. Not from a lòhren. And not from you, who say you are a lòhren, but aren't."

He stood in the shuffa and drew his sword. "Now speak! Twice you have lied to me, which lòhrens don't

129

do. Your staff isn't broken. That was your first lie. And you said you were heading in the direction of the Angle. That was your second. Now, speak truly. Why were you waiting by the lake, and who are you?"

The girl glared, her eyes boring right through him, but he did not flinch. At length, she smiled, or at least bared her flashing white teeth.

"Well, the young kitten has claws after all. But are you not afraid? I have lòhrengai at my command that could blast you to a cinder." As she spoke, flame played across her fingertips, ready to leap at her will.

"I mistrust magic," he said without hesitation, "but I don't fear it. I've faced it before, from greater threats than you, and survived."

She eyed him again for a long while, and a frown creased her face.

"Maybe you have."

Her words were calm, but the air was charged with tension. Anything could happen at any moment, and he could not read her except for a sense of bafflement. Nor, he suspected, could she read him. They were opposites, as unalike from each other as possible, and that was dangerous.

They stared at each other, unmoving, while fate and destiny swirled around them like currents in the misty air. Then suddenly she smiled, and it was genuine this time, though flame still darted and danced at her fingertips.

"Very well. You're right, but you're wrong also. I was drawn to Lake Alithorin. Don't ask me why, I don't know. I found myself studying the battle, though I knew that wasn't what drew me. And I saw no way to get through to the fortress to help anyway, and that confirmed my instincts. I was needed, but not for what was most obvious. A lòhren's feelings often work that way. A hunch, a momentary vision, a whim that turns

130

out to be something more. So I waited, unable to help the city, but unable to go either. I didn't know for what I was called until I saw you flitting through the trees, and a merry chase you gave me until finally I caught up. I can say no more than that. I acted on instinct, and it has never yet let me down."

He thought about her response, but never lowered the point of his sword. What she said had the ring of truth, but it did not really answer his most pressing question.

"Why did you lie about your staff? It isn't broken, that much I know, and a lòhren without a staff … isn't really a lòhren."

A shadow of remembered pain crossed her face.

"That isn't true. A lòhren doesn't need a staff. It just helps, and in the eyes of the people all across Alithoras it acts as a symbol. But the lòhrengai of a lòhren…"

She looked at him thoughtfully for a moment, and then changed what she was about to say. "All you need to know is this – I was a lòhren. I had a staff. And as you say, it wasn't broken. It was taken from me – taken away by the Lòhrenin, the council of lòhrens. Too deep I delved into forbidden lore. They thought I was turning down the paths of an elùgroth. At least so they feared." She gave a shrug. "Maybe they were right to stop me, maybe not. But no lòhren is the same as any other. Anyway, they would have expelled me from the order, but Aranloth persuaded them otherwise. They confiscated my staff, but they did not break it. For that, I owe him, and for other things beside. And I do not forget my debts. Had you killed him, you would not have seen this dawn. Yet still for five years they sent me away. Five long years, and only two have passed. When my punishment is ended, then I can return and they will judge me anew."

She said these last words with bitterness, and he glimpsed some of her great pride. And he understood also that she had no desire to tell him any of this, yet still, just as he had been forced to tell the truth before, so was she now. Fate or circumstance had caught them both in a tight grip. And just as he needed her help before, so now he knew that for some reason she would do anything to come with him to the Angle. But why?

She had not told him everything, but she had still told him much.

"And what of your second lie? You were not heading to the Angle or anywhere near it, until you knew that I was going there."

"That was no lie. It's true that I didn't intend to go there, but when you said that you would, then I knew that I must also. It is, as I said, what I've been waiting for. I didn't *know* what I was waiting for, or where I would end up going, but when you said that you must go there, and why – well, that was where I was going too. There was no lie in that."

She stared at him again, but this time it was not in anger, and when she spoke he felt that she was trying to tell him something different than what her words said.

"It's true that lòhrens don't lie. And maybe I've erred in telling you that my staff was broken. Maybe so, but a lòhren can weave greater deceptions by far, and yet still tell the truth."

He did not understand what she was getting at, but there were more important things to discuss.

"Tell me why you want to help," he asked. "You owe Aranloth, which I can understand. But why help *me*?"

"Because Aranloth would want me too. And I *do* owe him. But more is at stake than one city. All of Alithoras stands upon the brink. This is not the only battle. And there are other forces in the world besides swords…"

She had told him precious little. Then again, how much did she know and understand herself? A lòhren's intuition she had said. Perhaps he should just accept that, and her help. Certainly he needed it, but only if he could trust her.

Time was slipping away. He must be up and going, for the Angle was far away and the elugs and sorcerous beasts would find his trail sooner or later. The faster he moved now, the greater his lead would be, but on foot he could not count on keeping things that way.

The girl stared at him, assessing him even as he assessed her. The moments flitted by, and he knew he could not stand here talking all day until he learned and considered every detail of what was going on. He must either trust her, or not.

15. Troubled Sleep

Brand felt the weight of the sword in his hand. He also felt responsibility, and it was heavier. He and the girl faced each other, both ready to spring to defend themselves if necessary.

And yet both hesitated. Neither wanted a fight, that much was obvious. What Brand wanted, he knew in full. What she wanted, he knew only in part. And yet her words came back to him: she trusted in her instincts.

So must he. Whatever she was hiding, and he was certain that she was hiding more than one thing, he did not think she meant him harm. Or anyone else, for that matter, however abrasive her attitude.

Also, though he might part with her here if he chose to, she was obviously powerful, and would help him at need. And no greater need had he ever had, for to fail in this quest was to doom the king he served, and also Aranloth and the friends he had made. And an entire city.

What would Aranloth want him to do? Dare he risk taking this strange girl into the tombs with him? Had she even offered that? And what about revealing the charm Aranloth had taught him to protect himself once inside? He saw no way that he could keep that secret from her. Yet they were words that the lòhren had kept back even from Gilhain.

He had no answers, and he shrugged to himself. Sometimes, there *were* no answers. But he looked one last time into her eyes, and her gaze held his own unflinching.

He slowly sheathed his sword. "I'm Brand," he told her.

A moment longer she looked at him, and then the flame at her fingertips died away as she understood his choice.

"I'm Kareste," she answered. She held out her hand and he shook it. It was warm to touch as it had been before, although the fire was gone.

"We'd better move swiftly," she said.

They came to the shore in haste and hid the shuffa as best they could in some reeds. Brand doubted that he would ever see it again, yet he still looked around him and memorized the place. The future was dark, and unexpected need might drive him back here.

But it was likely the enemy would find it, if and when the beasts sniffed out their trail again.

Without any more words they headed off. Kareste led, setting a long loping pace that he could match, though it was still fast, and the day ahead of them long.

Swiftly the pine forest thickened around them again. Whatever sun rose in the east was hidden here. It remained a world that belonged to the night. The gray trunks of the trees were still – they seemed as statues in some ancient city. The fog was all about them, though not particularly thick. The needle-like leaves of the pines dripped moisture, slow but sure as the loping strides of the two runners, the only things that moved in the eerie shadow world.

On they went. Morning passed, if morning it was, and noon eventually came, revealed only by a lifting of the fog and the distant sounds of birds rather than an increase of light. Where they were it remained in perpetual dark, but the ground was soft with the needles of many years and the paths of some forest animal were clear. The running was good, and the walking better

135

when they slowed to rest. For few could run all day without stopping. And even if they could, they would not be fit to fight should they need to if discovered by their enemies.

So time passed, and they spoke little, but they travelled with a greater sense of comradeship and understanding.

There were times when words were unnecessary, and this was one to Brand. He had made his decision, and he would not worry about her any longer. His mind was bent on one thing alone now: to put as much distance between him and his enemies as he could. And to this end she led him well, for she ran swift as a deer when need demanded but loped like a wolf with mile eating strides, hour after hour. She was fitter than he was, more used to running. Or else she sustained herself by the power of lòhrengai that she commanded, yet Aranloth had told him that lòhrens shunned such uses of the art, relying on it as only a last resort, and that was one of the things that separated them from elùgroths who used it without discrimination, heedless of the consequences in the pursuit of short term gain.

Without warning they burst from the shadows of the forest onto sunlit grass. Kareste slowed and came to a stop. He drew up beside her. The sun was blindingly bright above, and the grass seemed brilliant green. The sky was a cooler and deeper blue than he ever remembered. So it seemed to him to see these things for the first time after the long dark, and his spirit swelled within him.

"Evil cannot endure forever. Not in the face of this," he said.

She raised an eyebrow. "Spoken like a true Duthenor tribesman."

She did not say it with malice, but still he was taken aback.

"I haven't told you that I'm of the Duthenor. How did you know?"

She did not hesitate. "It's my job to know these things. You speak well, almost as a native of Cardoroth, but still I hear the slow tongue, deep and rolling of the Duthenor, in your every word."

"You've been among my people?"

"I've been many places in Alithoras. Even to the wild lands of the Duthenor and the ancient homelands beyond where once the Camar dwelt before they came east and founded realms."

"And how do things stand among the Duthenor? I have heard no news in years."

At this she gave him a strange look. "How long has it been?"

"I'm older than I seem," he answered. "It's been some while."

"Then know this. The Duthenor chieftain is not well liked. Yet the people have little choice but to obey him and suffer his rule. Other tribesmen, not of the Duthenor, support him. They are related, but are not like your people. They are warriors, fell and fierce, without pity or morals."

"Do the Duthenor not revolt?"

"That they have done. But the chieftain is as ruthless as the strangers he invited in to help him. It led only to blood and death. They endure his rule now, waiting for a time they believe will come."

"What time is that?"

"The time when the trueborn chieftain returns."

There was a pause. Brand did not speak, and she looked at him with eyes that seemed to read his every secret. If he did not believe she was one of Aranloth's kind before, he believed it now.

"Perhaps the trueborn chieftain will one day return. If so, the Duthenor must yet wait a while. But it's good to hear tell of my people. And know this. They are patient. They *will* endure. But they do not forget. He who assumed the chieftainship by murder may sleep in the long hall that he stole, but he does not sleep well. Distrust and suspicion surround him during the day, fear assails him at night. For justice will prevail, and for every act of treason there is a price. He dreads that, and he'll one day learn that his fears are well founded."

Kareste gazed at him with the eyes of a lòhren. She knew much, guessed more, but revealed nothing of her thoughts by her expression.

They paused where they were for a while, resting in the last cover of the forest where its eaves gave way to the grasslands.

"We have a choice," she said, sitting down with her back to a tree. "The lands are wide and empty between here and the Angle. Our enemies roam them with freedom, though they are mostly concentrated around Cardoroth."

"There may be enemies ahead," he said. "But there are sure to be enemies behind, also."

She rested the back of her head against the tree trunk. "I've not forgotten them. And our journey must be on foot, which will make it hard to avoid them, either those before or those behind."

"What of the country that we have to traverse? What's it like?"

She closed her eyes. "The Great North Road, which is not that far away, is flat and smooth. It would speed our journey, at least the beginning of it, but it's impossible to hide there. The other way, direct across the land, will reduce the miles we must travel, but it'll be slower going for hills, woods and streams will hinder us. But those same things will also provide cover."

Brand made his decision quickly. "We should go that way," he said. "The land is our friend, in all its varied forms. An open road in the wild is no place to meet the beasts that come after us."

"No place is good for that," she said.

They did not linger long, but soon struck out again across the grass. Of the enemy, there was no sign, but still Brand felt vulnerable in the open. Yet there was no choice in what they did, and to wait until the cover of nightfall was more dangerous still.

The afternoon waned, and it grew dark. He was weary as he had rarely been before, and even Kareste showed signs of tiredness, she who seemed proof against danger, peril and exhaustion. But neither of them had slept for a long while, and many hard miles lay in their wake.

They sat beneath a lone pine that towered into the sky. It was, perhaps, the last remnant of a once larger forest that had grown around Lake Alithorin and shrunk over time through the damage of successive waves of migrating men. Or maybe it was the first thrust of the forest to conquer new lands and cover them with a mass of dark-leaved trees. He did not know, but the old needles that lay thick beneath it were a soft place to sit and rest.

They ate little and spoke less. But it was a comfortable silence, and it enabled him to think. Night crept from the dark band of the forest now far away, but it rolled ever more swiftly over the grasslands and soon swamped all in its vast blanket.

The stars sprang like sparks from a forge into the blackened sky, and he looked up at bright Halathgar. The two glittering points shone at him like seeking eyes. They looked down also on Cardoroth, and he wondered what was happening there. And lastly, he considered that they also gazed on the lands of the Duthenor far away.

What was happening to his own people? The Careth Nien, the Great River, offered them some protection against the hordes of elugs that had come into the north. The river was not easy to cross. He knew that better than most. And it would be harder for armies than a lone man, but still they were at risk. Now, more than ever, he wanted to be with them. But his task in these foreign lands was not yet done.

At length he fell into a deep sleep. He found rest in oblivion, and ease from his many cares and worries, but it did not last. They lit no fire and it grew cold. The leaves were not so soft as he had thought, and the roots of the tree formed hard ripples in the earth. He dreamed that they rose up and took hold of him, shaking him fiercely.

He stirred, coming to wakefulness with a wrench, and found that the roots were just where they should be, but that there *were* hands on him nonetheless, and they *did* shake him.

It was Kareste, and even in the dimness beneath the great tree he saw the expression on her face. It was one of great urgency.

"They come," she said.

And he knew what she meant, for even as she spoke the beasts that had hunted in silence through the forest, seeking to take their prey by stealth, now howled in frenetic glee as they followed a warm scent.

16. Called from the Otherworld

Brand leaped up, grabbed his pack and strapped it on. Without further delay, the two of them loped off.

"We need cover and height," she said.

Brand did not answer. She was right, but even as she spoke their boots trod ground that led them on a steeper grade. They did not see it so much as feel it, but they followed the rise in the land and hoped that somewhere ahead in the dark was cover.

This proved to be the case. As they ran, trees grew up about them. They were not pines this time, but rather some kind of shrubby evergreen. The cover was not great, and Brand felt in his heart anyway that their time of hiding was over. The time for fighting was near.

They reached the crest of the rise. It could hardly be called a hill, and the shrubby growth about them dispersed rather than grew denser. From their vantage they saw the black shadows of night spread out below them, yet the sky was gray and the stars fading even as they looked. He might yet see one last dawn, but after that, hope would dwindle swiftly.

Even as they looked behind them they saw five creatures race amid the trees. The noise of thrashing branches and the crashing of large animals through underbrush came to them loudly in the otherwise peaceful dark.

And then they heard once more the beasts give rise to their baying din. This time they did not howl. Instead, they voiced deep and bellowing barks.

Brand looked ahead at something that he had seen earlier. Boulders littered the crest of the rise. They would not help much, but they offered some advantage, and he would take what he could get at the moment. He did not need to say anything to Kareste. They both ran for them at the same moment.

They leaped onto the largest, clambering over its rough surface until they reached the top, though it was little more than six feet above ground level. Within moments the beasts raced across the grass toward them, tufty fur prickled in rage or excitement, red tongues lolling from slavering jaws.

The beasts drew close, snuffling and snarling as they circled the boulder. Not yet did they attempt to climb it or leap; they were wary, considering with an intelligence beyond animals what was to be done next.

Kareste hissed as she studied them.

"Foul summonings. Dredged from the darkest pits of sorcery. Yet sorcery is not the only power in the world."

Brand watched them closely also. Where skin showed, not covered by the bristly fur, the muscles beneath rippled with size and strength beyond any beast he had seen before. These things were not quite hounds, and they were not quite wolves. They looked back at him with an expression that unnerved him. He saw malice, and believed that his earlier fears were founded.

"Are these creatures part man?" he asked Kareste, not taking his eyes from their roving forms.

"Of course," she replied. "They're called from the otherworld, but held in place by the transformed bodies of men."

"The elùgroths sacrificed some of their own soldiers?"

She shrugged. "These are more valuable to them than any soldiers. The staff is their greatest concern, greater

142

even than taking Cardoroth. It wouldn't surprise me if one or more sorcerers came after the beasts. We're lucky that they ran ahead of the hunt, though the rest cannot be far behind. Men, elugs and elùgroths all."

Brand looked around. He saw nothing else but the hounds. These still circled below, biting and snapping and growling. Suddenly, one leaped high. It scrambled over rock, the great forepaws heaving its vast bulk upward like a man climbing a ladder.

Kareste did not hesitate. Flame, blue as the midnight sky, roared from her fingers and smashed into it.

The creature howled and dropped off the boulder, but it merely lumbered into the shadows and glared at her with bared lips. It did not die.

That was a shock to Brand. He did not expect her powers to obliterate the creatures instantly, but he saw clearly that they would not be enough. The beasts could be hurt by lòhrengai, but killing them all would take time. And of that they had little.

Even as the beast snarled at them from a safe distance, the others drew closer, studying the boulder and analyzing the situation for a better way to attack.

And in the distance, the new-risen sun shone golden light on the last thing Brand wanted to see. Azan riders. Light flared from their naked swords, and it flashed from spears and polished helms. Yet there were only six, and that gave him hope, and the spark of an idea.

He shivered, part in fear and part in excitement. Whatever was to be done must be done soon. Otherwise, more and more of the hunt would gather.

He looked at Kareste, tall and proud and calm on the top of the boulder.

"We need those horses," he said

She returned his gaze. "Yes we do. But are you mad? We have to worry about the hounds first. They're a greater threat than the riders."

"We can't delay. Others will likely soon come. Either hounds or elugs or elùgroths. We cannot wait any longer."

"Wait for what?" she asked.

But Brand did not answer.

17. Not for Nothing

Brand remembered the words of Aranloth. *The staff will help you.* He had no magic of his own, yet the staff did. His question was, how much did he trust the lòhren? For surely he could not attack the beasts with his blade. He would need more than that to survive against them.

Kareste still looked at him questioningly, unable to guess what he was about to do. He sheathed his blade, shook off his pack and smiled at her fiercely. The thrill of battle pumped in his veins. And then, without warning, he turned and leaped from the boulder into the very midst of the hounds.

The girl screamed. It was a sudden cry of shock and fear. It pierced the air and brought all eyes to her. All except for Brand's.

He landed lightly, even as the hounds turned toward him. He spun among them, smelling their fetid breath and hearing up close their throbbing growls. The very earth beneath his boots seemed to thrum to their deep-throated rumbling and the padding of their massive paws.

But he did not wait for them to attack. They were as shocked as Kareste had been, and that was the moment of opportunity he hoped for. Fortune favored the bold.

Aranloth's staff sang as he swung it. With all the strength of his will he brought it down upon the skull of the nearest beast. To his surprise, there was a flash of magic. It sputtered to life, and he felt a strange power tingle through his body and flare in the timber. After a faltering moment, as though of a kindled flame that

145

might yet be snuffed out, it roared in a fury of fire that blazed like the sun, though the light was silver, shot through with blue.

He nearly dropped the staff. The hound leaped in pain and surprise. It landed, stumbling and disorientated. With a howl it thrashed in rage as fire caught in the great ruff of fur around its neck, sending curls of putrid smoke into the air.

The beast shambled away, howling and rolling in the grass to try to put out the flame that burned it. The other hounds held back, growling. A moment they studied him, uncertainty in their eyes.

That moment was all he needed. He was off, sprinting straight at the horsemen. He saw from their faces that they did not believe what he had just done. With luck, it would take them a few seconds to realize what he would do next.

All was caught in a net of confusion and surprise, and he was at the center of it. But the hounds, after their initial reticence, bounded after him. Brand feared they would reach him before he could accomplish his true aim, but just then he heard a wild yell from behind.

Kareste had left the safety of the boulder, and with the hounds before her, oblivious to what she did, she sprayed blasting fire among them.

He saw the streaking light flicker all through the air, heard the yelps of pain and noticed the pounding chase falter and grow disordered.

Before they grasped what was happening, Brand was among the horsemen. Their steeds were wild with fear, both from the nearing beasts and the sudden flame. They bucked and kicked and screamed with fright.

Some of the men lifted their swords, and the bright blades flashed as they swept toward him. But he was fleet of foot, and they must also try to control their mounts and avoid falling.

He blocked a vicious cut that came too near, but this time Aranloth's staff did not flare with lòhrengai. It seemed that only the sorcerous beasts triggered it, or something else entirely. But he needed no magic. He was better skilled at fighting than these warriors, and he knew exactly what he intended, whereas they were still in shock at being attacked in the most unlikely circumstances.

He waited for just the right moment when the weight of one of the horses shifted and the rider was fighting for balance, and then he struck with the point of his staff, thrusting the man from his saddle to land with a heavy thud. In a moment he had dislodged yet another rider.

He ducked beneath a wild slash, and then grabbed the loose reins of the nearest riderless horse and jumped into the saddle.

The mare bucked and kicked, but he held on. He realized that it was not trying to dislodge him. Rather, it lashed out in fear. For the hounds were among the riders now. Some aflame, but all maddened and confused. And all driven by their sorcerous instinct to attack.

The Azan men that he had pulled from their horses came to their feet, but they were too slow to realize their danger and react. The hounds were upon them, driven by pain and frenzy, and they pounced at what was nearest to them.

The Azan screamed. The hounds mauled them. Blood spurted and bones cracked. It was too much for the remaining Azan. They kicked their mounts into a gallop and fled.

Brand struggled with his horse, but he managed to direct it away from the hounds and toward the second riderless horse. This spun and kicked, catching one of the hounds that mauled the men. He heard a thud that could only mean cracked ribs, and then the second lot of reins was in his hand and he was off.

He galloped back toward the boulders. Kareste was running toward him, ash-blond hair trailing in her wake and green-brown eyes on fire. Smoke curled from a swathe of burnt grass at her feet, and one of the hounds lay there, dead. It was a blackened thing. Fire smoldered in the deep fur at the ruff of its neck, but it had been burnt away from the rest of its body. Everywhere bright red blood seeped from the charred skin.

Kareste grabbed the reins of the second horse and mounted. Behind him, Brand heard a gut wrenching scream and a vicious snarl. The Azan were dead, and the beasts would now turn back to their proper prey.

They wheeled the horses round to face their enemy. The hounds looked at them. Blood smeared their snouts. Their lips curled back and low snarls rumbled in their throats.

At the same moment, Kareste lifted her hands and Brand his staff. Lòhrengai sprang to life, streaking across the gap and smashing into the beasts. It knocked two of them off their feet, concentrated on one and drove it back, rolling and tumbling until it lodged against a low bush.

Leaves flared. Fur caught alight. A frenzied series of yelps turned into a suddenly human wail. With a final blast of lòhrengai both beast and shrub burst into billowing flames like a bonfire.

The other beasts stood their ground. Brand pointed the staff at them and spurred his horse forward. This was become too much for them, and they turned and fled, racing back down the slope and into the cover of the trees.

All was still now atop the slope except for the burning shrub and what lay beneath it.

Brand looked at Kareste. She returned his gaze. They were both silent. Sweat dripped from them, cold on their skin although the sun shone warmly from the clear blue sky.

At length, Kareste nudged her mount closer and spoke.

"Not for nothing did Aranloth choose you. And though you distrust magic, there is more to you than meets the eye. Mine at least. Aranloth, obviously, saw more clearly. But still … you *are* mad."

He smiled at her again, filled with exuberance.

"Maybe so. But I'm alive, and if you want to stay that way – follow me!"

That his words were an echo of her own were bound to annoy her, but he did not care. She deserved that little rebuke, not that anything mattered now except that the quest might still be fulfilled.

He gathered up his pack and they sped off, both riders and mounts happy to leave the slope behind them. It stunk of sorcery, death and fear, and it would take many days of open air and bright sunlight to make it otherwise.

The long strides of the horses made easy work of the hill, which soon angled downward, and they pounded to its bottom and then raced away even faster on the level ground beyond.

Of the hunt, Brand did not yet see any sign. But it would regroup. Others would join and strengthen it. The pursuit would not falter, for the trail it must follow was clear and scent was no longer needed.

The beasts could be killed. That was heartening. So also was the fact that he and Kareste were now mounted. That would lengthen the chase, but he did not doubt that sooner or later their enemy would catch up with them. That did not matter so much, even if there were elùgroths next time, so long as he first obtained Shurilgar's staff and destroyed it. If he accomplished the quest, nothing else really mattered. He just hoped that Kareste had left him by that point. Alithoras was vast, and they would not pursue her if they found him first.

18. A Great Darkness

They rode warily but with great speed. The sun arced above them, bringing ever greater warmth and light to wash away some of the horror of their encounter with the beasts.

But Brand knew he would never forget the hounds that looked at him with the calculating eyes of a man. Worse, he guessed that it was not the last time that he would see them, or their kind.

He felt fear and determination in equal parts. Fear, because the creatures were made of evil and bent on his death. Determination, because such atrocities should not be allowed to walk Alithoras. The elùgroths and the dark powers at their command must be stopped. Fate had given him an opportunity to help with that, and it was more important than his personal goal among the Duthenor. And, in the end, what helped Cardoroth also helped his own people, even if they did not know what he was attempting, nor ever would learn of it.

They rode and rested and rode again. The day passed, and night came after with a shimmer of stars. Yet darkness did not stop them. On they went, oftentimes walking the horses to give them relief, at other times just urging them forward at a gentle trot. But ever they went on, striving toward their goal.

And *their* goal he now thought it, for though the danger and obligation to reach the tombs was his, Kareste had shared in the risk so far and become a companion rather than a stranger met along the way. She had stood by him when he needed it, and he would do the same for her. Loyalty was like trust, he thought: swiftly earned but impossible to regain once lost. But she had both his loyalty and his trust.

Brand studied her as they traveled, but she veiled herself and her thoughts. Not lightly did she give her own trust, and even less easily did she make friends. Yet the abrasiveness that was in her when they first met was gone. Something had made her angry then, perhaps that she helped the cause of the lòhrens even when they shunned her. But now the two of them were getting to know each other, and he did not think that she held anything against him any longer.

He scratched the skin of his forehead beneath Aranloth's diadem. The metal ornament was warm to touch, and he wondered for the first time what power it held. For it seemed to him that he had greater insight into Kareste's thoughts and motives than he would have expected. But he did not really believe that any lòhrengai could do that. Such intuition as he had came through his experiences, both the good and the bad. No artifact could substitute for that. Life must be lived, people known through both good and hard times to understand why they did what they did. No diadem could replace that, no matter if it was imbued with magic.

Well into the night they finally slept. And a deep slumber it was, for pursuit or no, hounds or not, they must rest. Yet they woke with the dawn and sped away again.

The lands they now travelled seemed strange to him. He had heard rumor of them, and had it described to him by Aranloth, but still the country was different from what he knew. There were few trees, and what hills there were marched far away and seemed bare rather than choked by tree and bush. He guessed it likely that he had become the best travelled of all the Duthenor that ever

152

lived, for his feet had trod the eastern side of the Great River, led him up north to the verge of the northern mountains that lured him so, and now he rode south into lands beyond the dominion of Cardoroth. He supposed they were still Gilhain's lands, yet the king was far away, as were his soldiers, and if any people lived here they were brave homesteaders, recking little of kings and cities, and trusting in the hidden ways of forest, hill and valley to hold them safe from enemies.

"You haven't been here before?" Kareste asked him.

Brand shook his head. "Aranloth told me something of the area, but that's not the same."

"No, it's not. So in case we get separated, I'll tell you what I know."

She was silent for a moment, deciding best how to describe things. Then she pointed with her long right arm.

"Quite a few miles to our right is the Great North Road, made by the Halathrin long ago. It's still a good road, and it runs straight and true." She glanced at him. "You must have crossed it further north when you came to Cardoroth."

He nodded, and she continued. "The road drives deep into the south, much further than we'll go. It reaches to the crossings of the Carist Nien river, and even well beyond that to the Careth Nien, more than a hundred leagues away, nigh to the borders of the forest realm of the Halathrin. Also to the right, beyond the Great North Road, are the hills of Lòrenta. There stands the keep of the lòhrens – secure against enemies, sorcerous or otherwise, though few guard it. It isn't protected by swords, but by powers older and stronger than iron and steel."

She shifted in her saddle and swept an arm out to the left. "Some fifty miles that way lies the sea."

Of the sea, Brand had heard many stories. But he had never seen it. Vast it must be if Lake Alithorin was as a puddle beside it, as some in Cardoroth had told him. Yet pearls he had looked at once, on a necklace of his mother's, and they were said to come from it. And once a twisted shell which had come from some strange creature. His father had held it to his ear and told him that the strange sound he heard, the soft and undulating roar, was the sound that the great waters made as they surged and flowed. Well he remembered those words, though he was very young, and he wanted to see the truth of it.

Kareste went on with her description, and he listened, entranced by her every word.

"When we reach the Carist Nien, if not sooner, we must turn east and follow it in that direction, toward the sea. Thence we'll come at length to the Angle – the home in ancient days of an empire that crumbled to dust ere either Camar or Duthenor wandered out of the dark into the brighter lands of the east and founded chieftainships and after realms."

As she spoke, her words evoked the history and the wonder of the land, but he sensed also that forces were at work within it. The lòhrens and their allies on one hand, and the elùgroths, elugs and Azan on the other. Far to the south was the home of their enemies, beyond the Careth Nien, beyond green Galenthern, which was but a rumor to him, beyond the Graèglin Dennath mountains that tales of legend spoke of, and then, in a far country, Grothanon, whence the great powers of the enemy dwelt.

Of other cities that lay between he had heard some names: Faladir, Menetuin, Camarelon. But there were once other cities, fallen to the enemy, as also would Cardoroth if his quest did not succeeded. If it did, then perhaps they had a chance, for the wiles of the king were great, and many bold hearts wielded swords with hope and defiance.

They rode ever on. Kareste was often quiet beside him, withdrawn into some world of her own. What troubled her, he did not know. Perhaps what surely followed after them. Perhaps what lay ahead. Maybe something else entirely.

And then on other days she was suddenly happy, as though the sun burst through clouds on a rainy day. He was not sure what to make of her, but he was growing to like her better and better. Certainly, she was unlike the girls of his homeland, and unlike the girls of Cardoroth as well.

A great darkness lay behind her, and he guessed her life had not been easy. That she hid much, he knew, but he trusted her more and more. He supposed, thinking about things honestly, that it would seem to her that he also hid much. So he did, and she did not press him, so the least he could do was offer her the same grace.

But one day, when a gray veil of drizzle covered the land and she seemed talkative, he asked her a question. She would either respond or not, and he would not press her.

"You're not from Cardoroth," he said. "Where do you come from?"

She hesitated, deciding whether or not to answer him. She was, he guessed, coming to like him and more inclined to talk. So he hoped, but at the same time the thought was unsettling.

"Am I not from Cardoroth?" she answered. "Well, perhaps not, although I did live there once. But before that, *long* before that, some few people from that city sought out new lands, well away from the rule of the king – not the current king, and the trammeled ways of stone and gate and city streets. They trekked north, settling at last along the Alith Nien river that feeds Lake Alithorin. There they fished and tilled the fertile soils to either side of the river. It was a good life, but a hard one. But the fish were plentiful, and the harvests of grain and fruit were good. Thus also, dwelling where they did, they became skillful with boats – the crafting of them as well as the using of them. But there were hunters among them too, for meat was ever scarce even when the crops were good."

Her horse picked its way through some broken rocks and she gave it free reign to do so, absent-mindedly watching the ground as she spoke.

"And the hunters travelled far, seeking ever new lands where the game was less shy of men and the hunting that little bit easier. They strayed even under the shadow of the northern mountains, Auren Dennath as they're called in the Halathrin tongue, and some few followed ridges and dim forest paths, hunting higher and higher, ever nearer to the snow-mantled peaks."

He listened to her as she spoke, feeling once again that tremor of excitement that shivered his body when he heard the name of those mountains, Auren Dennath, the high lands that he had seen from a distance but never climbed. But he asked her no questions about them, fearing to interrupt, for she spoke so seldom of anything that mattered to her, and he felt also that what she said now touched on the darkness that lay behind her. Especially since he had wandered over the lands on either side of that river before coming to Cardoroth, and had never met any people nor seen sign of them.

"Fair they thought those mountains, and the hunting was good, so more and more of them went there. But after a time, none returned. So it happened that my people were discovered, for elugs dwelt there of ancient days, though not in great numbers. Yet their roaming bands were enough. They gathered together one wet autumn, and falling upon our folk slew them – men, women and children. Only a handful lived. Of these, I was one. And I too would have died save for Aranloth." She shuddered. "I was very young. And very scared. Too young to remember much, and too scared to want to. But I'll never forget the fire and smoke and great lights, and Aranloth standing there, alone and unaided, defying a band of elugs. They retreated, and he scooped me up and took me to Lòrenta. There were none that I knew there, either young or old, for the few others who survived went to Cardoroth."

She paused for a moment, and when she went on her voice held a new note.

"But I didn't forget my past. Against the elugs I hold a grudge, for they took my childhood from me, and more. Yet Aranloth gave me a new life, and ever was I keen to learn the ways of power, for he trained me as a lòhren, and this I became. But whereas the others my age spent their time learning how to heal, and to offer counsel and succor to the needy, and power last, I turned in a different direction. Power I would have, and I would have it as swiftly, and as much of it as I could get, to defend against enemies."

Here then was the beginning of how she fell afoul of the Lòhrenin. He could not really blame her, and it comforted him that Aranloth had stood up for her, and in that lòhren's judgement he trusted completely.

Yet he noted that she said little of *what* powers she sought, and what she would do with them if gained, other than the vague comment of *defend against enemies*. That could mean just about anything.

Whatever else, he guessed that she had made good on that desire and acquired many skills, a few of which he had seen. What exactly she intended to do with them, and what dark lore she had delved into that had forced the lòhrens to cast her out, even if only for a time, were other problems. But if problems they were, they were not to be solved now, if ever they could be.

19. Beyond the Reach of Thought

It felt to Gilhain that he now lived on the Cardurleth.
He dared not leave it, for the attacks of the enemy did
not let up. And he trusted to no other to organize the
defense. Not that others were incompetent; there were
many who could do the task, but the responsibility was
his alone.

Aurellin, his wife, spent much time with him. Little
love she had for battle, but her temperament was always
calm, and though unskilled in arms herself she had a
store of knowledge on warfare that would put a general
to shame. He relied on her as much as them, if not more,
but still so many decisions were his alone, and they
weighed him down.

He was getting old now. His mind retained its agility,
but his body constantly let him down. If he survived this,
if Cardoroth survived this, he was reaching a point where
he must either abdicate his throne or else hold on, old
and infirm, while his enemies within the city, and
perhaps those outside such as his half-brother, plotted
against him. That would not help Cardoroth. But it was a
problem that he must put aside, even though it weighed
increasingly heavy upon him.

Aurellin was by his side, as usual, when the new day
of battle began. He glanced at her but did not speak. As
the years went by he found they conversed less, not
because their love faltered, but because they knew each
other so well. She smiled back at him, a weary attempt,
and her eyes were shadowed, for she guessed at what he
now thought. Their time together was drawing to an end.

She was younger than he, and they both wanted to spend what years were left away from war and trouble and the rule of a great city that would burden even a young man.

Aranloth was there too. The lòhren never seemed to rest. He had a kind word here for a wounded soldier, a helping hand there to those in need, and he remained ever a source of courage and humor when these things were required.

He was a better strategist than Gilhain was himself, but he never put himself forward, always offering humble advice, and allowing Gilhain to lead. For this much was true: Cardoroth had trust in their king. Even now, after so long a siege, they seemed little worried. They waited for some grand stroke of his that would break the enemy. Only he did not have one. What hope they had he had already placed in Brand.

He thought about the lòhren. He gave no commands, yet his influence was everywhere. Aurellin was here because she wanted to be, yet that was Aranloth's idea first. It was true that she did not wish to be parted from him. It was true that she also gave heart to the men, for she was much loved and respected. But Gilhain knew that Aranloth had encouraged her presence to help put his mind at rest. If his wife was away in the palace, he would always worry of some sorcerous attack that might be made against her. That would break him, but here at least, with Aranloth constantly by both their sides, he did not fear that, and he was free to think only of the daily attacks against the wall.

And though no further attacks had been made directly at him, still the sorcerous chanting during the night continued. But it was directed at the whole city. It was like a soul-sapping dirge: depressing, bleak and used with the elug chant to lower the morale of the defenders.

So things had been for a seemingly endless series of days, though in truth it was not that long. Yet today was different. They all sensed it, most especially Aranloth who had been uneasy since yesterday afternoon, and that tenseness grew over the long night.

Other lòhrens moved along the walls. Their white robes gleamed, and they shifted their staffs from hand to hand. It was a rare sign of nerves.

"What is it?" Gilhain asked, turning to his old friend.

Aranloth slowly shook his head as though coming back from somewhere far away.

"I don't know. *Something*. Something that the enemy hasn't tried before. This much I can say – there's a change in the air. I feel it. The other lòhrens feel it. Even some of the men sense it. But what it is … I don't know."

Gilhain knew what he meant. There was a brooding menace to the air like a storm in the distance: building, growing, massing – but not yet ready to break. But when it did break, and that felt inevitable, it would not be with wind and rain and hail.

He studied the dark host below. He cast his gaze around its perimeter. He considered its center, scrutinizing elugs, men and Lethrin with his experienced gaze. But he learned nothing.

For whatever reason, the enemy had also ceased the chanting. Normally that would be welcome, but just now he was not so sure. Nothing made sense today, and that worried him more than anything.

What was he missing? Was there something that he could do, or was the attack now moving beyond strength of arms and the courage of brave hearts to something that only lòhrens could defy?

The morning ran its course. As usual, the attacks began, but he knew they were half-hearted. The elugs were driven forward by their masters, climbing the walls in a dull stupor, knowing that they ran and climbed to their deaths. It was clear to both sides that those who sent them did not send enough, nor did they support them with archers or the beat of war drums.

The attacks were easily beaten off by the soldiers on the wall. Men laughed and joked. They leaned on their spears or the stonework, talking freely and enjoying this turn of events. It was better than the desperate fighting for life against a maddened enemy imbued by rage to kill. But that only fuelled Gilhain's unease all the more.

At noon, the enemy host grew quiet. No further sallies were made. Through its dark ranks paced a wedge of elùgroths. As a wave they came forward, the host parting for them, either in awe or fear for their lives.

Aranloth strained to look. And whether his sight was better than a normal man's, or he used some art of lòhrengai, he saw what Gilhain did not.

"Khamdar is not there."

They both guessed what that meant. "If he is not there," Gilhain said, "with his host at a time when they're obviously preparing for some great attack, then he has gone after Brand."

That scared him. If Brand was not dead, then soon he must face an enemy beyond his strength, for no man and few even among lòhrens could face an elùgroth, least of all one such as Khamdar.

"There's still hope," he said after a pause. "If Khamdar had caught and killed Brand, he would have returned to his host. His absence is, in a way, promising."

"Maybe," Aranloth said uncertainly. "But he might still be returning."

162

"That is so," Gilhain replied. "And yet if Brand still lives he must now be approaching the Angle and the last part of the quest. The staff is within his reach."

They said no more. The elùgroth wedge had stopped between the host and the wall. They sat, still dark statues as they seemed, their wych-wood staffs pointed at the Cardurleth.

The war drums began to beat again. The elug chant rose also, becoming one with them and they one with the words:

Ashrak ghùl skar! Skee ghùl ashrak!
Skee ghùl ashrak! Ashrak ghùl skar!

And then the elùgroths began to chant themselves. What words they uttered, Gilhain did not know. Yet their force reached out into the very air, stretched to the wall, sunk deep into the earth and soared into the heavens. The sun seemed darker. The air more chill. Elugs, drums, chanting and sorcery all worked to one dark purpose. That much he knew, but what it was he could not guess.

The air tingled. The sun dimmed further as though clouds veiled it, yet the sky was empty. A gusty wind came up from the south, tugging at banners, blowing dust in little whirlwinds and scattering dead leaves as though thrown by the hands of the enemy themselves, for there was spite in it, even if it did no damage.

Gilhain squinted against a slap of dust-filled air.

"What is it?" he asked again, hoping that this time Aranloth had an answer.

The lòhren did not reply at once. He stood straight and tall. If the wind and dust and driving leaves annoyed him, he showed no sign of it. His gaze remained fixed on the enemy as though nothing else in the world mattered. At that moment, it did not.

At length, Aranloth glanced back at him. It was strange to see him without diadem or staff, but one thing was unchanged. His eyes were those of a man who had seen tragedies unfold: the death of loved ones, the massacre of innocents and the fall of nations. Pain was in them, both remembered and expected.

"I do not know," he said hoarsely. "But it is something wicked beyond the reach of our thought."

20. Bright were our Swords

Brand and Kareste had long since turned eastward. They had reached, and now followed, the Carist Nien river. Somewhere ahead was the land that Aranloth called the Angle.

There was no sign of any pursuit, and he thought that strange. He glanced at Kareste, quiet as usual where she rode on his left.

"Do you think we've lost them?"

"Maybe. But there's another way to look at it. They may know where we go, and where Shurilgar's staff is secured. There's great power in it, and they will not allow it to be destroyed – if they can help it. Even better if they can obtain it for their own use. And no doubt it has many uses that neither Aranloth nor the elùgroths have considered…"

Brand did not like that new line of thought. "I don't see how they could know where we're going. And though elùgroths might set a trap, I don't think the hounds, intelligent as they are, would run ahead rather than pursue."

"That might be true, but don't forget the elùgroths created the hounds. They obey their commands, and no matter how keen the chase, if one of the masters was with them they would be held under their control."

That was likely enough, and the thought of the enemy being ahead of them was not a pleasant one. So it was that for the next several days they moved warily along the grassy trail they followed.

And trail it was, for even here in the wilds of Alithoras men had come and dwelt here, though there was no sign of them now. Yet their long-ago presence marked the land. The faint path they followed was only one such sign. Another was the presence of fruit trees. These had grown wild, the descendants of trees once cultivated but long since gone to seed. How long ago, Brand could not guess…

He took out and looked over the map that Aranloth had given him. It had seemed detailed in Cardoroth, but now it was scant of information.

It showed several entrances and exits to the tombs in case of need, but a particular path was marked in heavier outline: the one the lòhren had preferred. It was the shortest, and Brand had no desire to prolong his time underground.

The closer he got to the tombs the more real Aranloth's warnings became. There were things there that he had no wish to see and meet, yet if wishes were truths he would not be here, would never have come to Cardoroth and the chieftainship of his people would be his. Nor would his parents have been killed by an usurper.

Yet wishes were not truths, and as much as he wished that he could change things, doing so would now mean a loss to him. He would be a poorer person for never having met Aranloth or Gilhain, for dwelling in the great city of Cardoroth, nor, and the thought surprised him, would he have met Kareste.

The river to their right grew as the days passed. A mighty thing it was, yet still not so great as the Careth Nien, the great river of Alithoras. Yet this one was still too broad to cross, a massive sweep of water that drove all before it. And it gathered pace and hurried along its course now, for the land began to slope downward at a steeper angle.

One night came when the roar of the river was loud as they slept, and the next day they saw rocks in the water and furious white-foamed rapids.

"We are come close to the Angle now," Kareste said. And she had to talk loud to be heard over the toss and thrash of the waters.

The path was plainer here. In fact, he saw several paths, but they followed only one. This led down steeply now, but before it did Brand took one last look at the river. It surged ahead, spilling and floundering over a mighty waterfall in the distance. Waves crashed and foamed. Spray cascaded into the air, and through it all the sun shot rainbow rays that came and went, leaped and fell as swift as the water-mist of the river rose and swirled above the land.

Suddenly, Brand had a sense of how vast Alithoras was, how many treasures it contained. He had seen but a fraction of it, and a hunger woke in him to see more; to tread paths that no man before him had trod, to explore the valleys, to find his way through the green-lit forests, and most of all to climb the northern mountains, whatever their dangers and look down on the land that the Halathrin had named Alithoras – the silver land, the land that even the immortals thought fair.

With slow steps he followed Kareste down the rocky path. Cliffs formed to his right, blocking out his view of the river. A great gorge opened up on the left, steep and shear, a drop so deep that it made him dizzy, and on the other side were more cliffs.

On the rock faces he saw at last the mark of the people who had once dwelt in these lands. No wild fruit trees grew here. This was mightier. This had endured through the ages intact, not seeding and growing and

167

seeding again through the long ages, but enduring wind and rain and sun and cold, enduring time itself. And if time had marred what once was there, time also had draped over it a sense of awe. For what he saw was carved by men, by men that had once lived and breathed as he did now, but who had died, according to Aranloth, some ten thousand years before. Yet still what they made spoke to him now with the freshness of a spell cast just at this moment. He looked. He saw, and the power of the magic, the power of time itself, smote him.

They both stopped together. Side by side they looked across the gorge and at the great figures in the rock on the other side.

A series of giant carvings were there, hundreds of feet high. The elements had blunted and cracked the images, but from this distance that was nearly invisible. There were bands of laborers working in unison to harvest wheat with sickle-shaped blades before they threshed the chaff from the grain. Nearby stood massive stone querns, turned by oxen to make flour. Hunters with keen spears, stealthy and silent, left a village with their heads lowered, searching for the spoor of game animals. There were miners, long-handled picks and shovels in the meaty hands, smiths and masons, dancers and storytellers. And there were warriors also. These were hard looking men in leather armor with round shields and short swords. And then Brand's eye was drawn to the largest carving of them all. He saw at the end of the long procession what must have been a king and queen. They were stern and fearful to look upon, and there was an edge of cruelty in their stony glance. They wore no crowns; instead, great diadems encircled their brows, such as the one he wore upon his own head.

Brand had never seen anything like it before, and the age of it, the greatness of it, took his breath away. All that work must have taken decades, even hundreds of years, to carve into hard rock.

Neither he nor Kareste spoke. At length, with a simple glance, she led him on once more. They went down the rough path that looked out over sharp-rocked death below and timeless beauty beyond.

The path was steep, and as they descended the roar of the waterfall lessened greatly. After a while, they came to a kind of recess where the ledge widened. That was as far as they could go because a rock fall blocked the way.

Brand studied it. It was not recent, but it did not seem old either. Nor was it natural. Some battle had been fought here, for the cliff above the rock was blackened by fire. Not the fire of burning timber, for there was none on this rocky slope, but of lòhrengai or elùgai. His battles were not the only ones in Alithoras.

But the rock fall was not the major point of interest. To the right of the recess was a kind of statue, and beyond that a cave. It was his first sight of the entrance to the tombs, and his heart sank. Even he, unskilled and void of magic, could sense the powers that dwelt within. There was malice there, a hunger for life and a will to bring death and destruction. Whatever waited inside was not his friend, nor the friend of any living thing.

Kareste looked at the statue, and he went over. At once he saw that it was a monument of some kind, rather than a statue.

"It's quiet here," he said. "I don't like it."

"It is ever thus," she answered. "This is a dead land. But even so, I know what you mean. It seems even stiller than normal."

"You've been here before?"

"Once. Long ago, it seems now."

"Have you been inside?"

She laughed at that, but it was a grim laugh. "No. None go in there. It is death."

"Then why do you think of doing so now? You don't have to, you know. In fact, I would prefer it if you didn't. This is my quest, and my responsibility. You've helped me greatly, and whatever debt you owe to Aranloth is paid."

She ran a hand through her long hair. "No, it is not paid. It can never be paid."

"Why not? You've saved my life, even as Aranloth saved yours."

"Because of many things…" Her voice trailed away.

It was no answer. But he knew he would get nothing more.

He looked around him, thinking. The recess they stood on was a large half-moon shape, perhaps forty feet long and just as deep at its furthest point. In the center sat a squat and ugly stone, the thing he had taken for a statue. It was as tall as he, but somewhat wider. Each of its four faces was carved with unusual writing.

He peered at it closely. The marks were a series of slashes, dots, and half circles, evidently some kind of writing, but it differed greatly from anything he had seen before.

"What does it say?" he asked.

Kareste rested her hand against the stone. "As you guess, it's the writing of the Letharn. It's an ancient thing. But as for what it says, it's better that you don't know."

"Words can't hurt me,' he said. "Tell me what they say."

Kareste shrugged. "So you say, but do you know all the secrets of the world, all the powers that battle to and fro, of which men hear only distant rumor? No, you don't. And it's better that way. But see the cave, there is writing there if you would have me translate it, though that too is a dangerous thing."

21. I am Death

Brand looked into the shadows around the mouth of the cave. It was buttressed by slabs of stone, and the high lintel was inlaid with the same curious writing. He looked back at her, and though he did not ask it, she read his will.

"Very well," Kareste said. She walked close. He followed, and when they stood near the entrance she spoke again. Her words were slow and halting, for he saw that she must translate the ancient script with care. But her voice, unhurried as it was, seemed more like a chant than anything else:

Attend! … We who mastered the world … are become dust. We possessed the wealth of nations. Gold adorned our hands; priceless jewels our brows; bright were our swords. The world shuddered … when we marched! Now, our glory lies unheeded in the dark of the tomb. Servants … mutter secret words as they walk the hidden ways … Death and despair take all others!

She fell silent. A long time Brand considered the words. It was a warning, but warning or no he must go inside. He looked around. There was no sign of the hunt, which was just as well, for they could not take the horses in.

Kareste followed his lead when he finally moved and tied her reins to some jutting rocks after him. They did not look particularly secure, but it was the best place available.

"We won't be that long," he said.

Kareste grinned at him. "Or we'll stay in there for eternity – one or the other."

"You're a real laugh, you are," he said, but there was a smile, albeit nervous, on his own face.

"Neither of us will be laughing by the end," she warned.

Brand looked one last time up the rocky trail that they had come down. He saw nothing, and he heard nothing, but that only made him mistrust the unnatural quiet all the more.

He led the way into the cave. It was not long before he saw the first bones. They were ancient things, crumbling near to dust, and swords rested near them. He did not look closely.

The road led inward, but then swiftly dropped at a steep angle. This was the route that Aranloth had chosen, and Brand remembered the lòhren's description. He also ran the charm through his mind, but he saw as yet no reason to use it.

The mouth of the cave behind them was nothing more than a pale glow, but Kareste muttered some strange words and a mist rose from the floor near her feet. But it was no ordinary mist. It eddied and swirled and followed the two of them, going wherever they went and giving off a faint pulsing light.

The road was straight. Brand heard the faint slap of their boots, quiet as they tried to be. It took him some time to realize that there were other noises as well. There was a whispering presence somewhere in the dark with them.

He spoke Aranloth's charm, stumbling over it a little, used rather to hearing it in his mind than saying it out aloud.

Shapes reared up behind them, and he turned, but by the time he did so they had dispersed again, either unwilling to be seen as yet or mollified by the charm, though he spoke it so softly that even Kareste would not have heard the words properly.

As they went ahead, slowly, cautiously, peering both before them and behind them, they saw that the tombs themselves had started. No longer was it a cave that they walked through, but a tunnel shaped by men, and in it, and the many smaller side passages that ran from it, the Letharn had laid men, women and children to their long rest.

Alcoves lined the sides of every passage, filled with bones and pottery and the implements of everyday life. All were ancient, seeming so fragile that they might break into dust at a careless breath, and yet Brand could not help wonder about them. Here were people who had once lived and breathed. They had once cooked meals and eaten. They had raised families, suffered sorrow and joy. They were the same as him no matter the vast gulf of time that separated them. And one day, regardless of whether or not he fulfilled this quest, or reached his other goals in life, he too would be bones and dust, memories on a forgotten breeze long ago blown across the world.

His thoughts were sobering and depressing – even immobilizing. Yet determination and stubbornness coursed through him in reaction. He might not know what had happened before he was born. He might not know what would happen after he died, as surely he would, but the time in between was his. And a long life or a short, it was *his* to make of it what he would.

He walked ahead more briskly, and he did not look to the sides.

"Touch nothing," he whispered to Kareste. "Touch nothing at all, for Aranloth warned me there is poison on

174

everything. Deadly poison – enough to kill you within moments."

"I haven't seen anything worth taking. But don't worry, I won't touch a thing."

"Remember that, and hold to it, for later there is wealth that you will never have seen. At least so Aranloth told me."

"Do you believe everything he says, always?"

It was a strange question, and he wondered why she asked it.

"I like many, but I trust few. Aranloth is one. The king of Cardoroth another. I would trust my life to either of them."

There was a pause. "Indeed you have, and I did not say it was a bad thing. But it may turn out differently than you expect."

"Doesn't it always?"

She did not answer, but he saw in the dim light the white flash of her grin.

The tombs changed as they went ahead. Brand's gaze was drawn against his will to look. And what he saw began to stun him.

Here were no ordinary tombs of laborers and peasants, as before. He saw piled gold and gems and artifacts of everyday life for the privileged, carved, decorated and inlaid with jewels. They were things of great craft: the harness of horses, combs of ivory, harps of polished timber, still strung; and there were lutes and drums and dresses and candleholders. He saw many things that the living used, but the dead needed not. And he saw the dead also. The preserved dead, dried and withered by time, but still with faces and arms and legs, uncorrupted because of some art of the Letharn.

He looked ahead again, for the dead fascinated him, but in that fascination was a trap. Something else was in the tombs with them, and he could afford no distraction.

If the thing, or things, with them was not dead, then neither were they alive. The figures that he had seen before began to press unseen at his mind, and he knew that the trial had not yet even begun.

He looked behind, but they were not there. He looked ahead, but he saw no sign of them. Yet he heard their whisperings in his mind and felt the cold touch of their unfathomable thoughts.

Eventually, he slowed, and then stopped. He had come to a place that Aranloth had told him about, but no description could prepare him.

There was a great crack in the rock. Through the fissure that ripped across the floor ahead of them there bubbled up the sound of rushing water. But it was faint as though coming from a great distance. Yet the way was not blocked, for over the gulf a slim bridge leaped, decorated and carved with strange figures at each end and graciously arched in the middle.

Strange lights shone upon it. Not from above, but from below, and they shifted and turned amid the dark, throwing up a shimmer onto the bridge. And a pillar stood before it, writing of gold-inlay glimmering from its black stone.

"What does it say?" he whispered.

Kareste peered at it for a moment. "It says, in the language of the Letharn, dead as they are themselves: *Harak kur likkil, harak ben luluck.* This I know, for Aranloth favored me with lore that not all lòhrens learn. Few know what those words mean now, and few spoke them even in the elder days when the iron-gripped rule of the Letharn rested heavily across wide realms. But once those words meant something, frightening even the mighty ancients that often knew war but seldom fear. When they were uttered, so Aranloth told me, the strongest warrior would cringe, kings would bow their heads and queens would wail."

Brand looked at her, solemn and unflinching in the strange lights, and he did not look away.

She gazed back at him, perceiving that he was not afraid of words alone, and gave him the translation.

I am death. I will devour you.

Brand looked at her a moment longer. "Fitting words for such a place."

He turned back to the bridge and stepped upon it. It felt hollow beneath his feet, for the stone was not thick, and he pictured the yawning gap below. But he did not look.

They began to cross. The roaring of water in the deeps of the earth grew louder. A faint breeze played across his face, and the lights glimmered up into his eyes.

After a while he could resist no longer and looked over the edge. It was black down there, blacker than the midnight sky, and yet like the sky there were lights that sparked and shimmered. But unlike stars they moved and spun, wheeling and arcing amid the blackness.

"What are they?" he asked.

Kareste stared at them for a moment. "I don't know. Not even the lòhrens know all things. And if Aranloth knew, he never told me."

They went ahead. Reaching the other end of the bridge, they stepped out again onto the solid stone of the earth once more. Ahead, they saw now a crossroads.

The main path ran true and straight before them, disappearing swiftly into the dark. Two other ways, smaller and narrower, shot left and right.

Brand did not hesitate. "This way," he said, and he turned left as Aranloth had told him to do. But they did not get far. Almost immediately he looked back, his eyes drawn by some instinct that he did not understand, for he had heard no noise.

Upon the crest of the arched bridge he saw three figures. The strange lights from the fissure below them flared, shining now many times brighter. Brand looked, and he saw, but he did not believe what he beheld.

Three women stood there. Three beautiful women. They were naked. Long hair streamed from proudly held heads. They gazed at him with sharp eyes, eyes that could bore through greater dark than that gathered even here in the tombs. They wore no ornament, not even the least of rings. But in their long-fingered hands they each held wicked knives: curved, serrated, designed to rend with pain and then draw forth intestines when pulled out of a victim's body.

And then, beyond his understanding, beyond anything he could have anticipated, they began to sing. It was a sound so strange, so unexpected, and yet all the more beautiful because of that.

He listened, entranced. And as he did so the figures seemed to grow. Tall they stood, their long hair shimmering in the strange lights, and their keen eyes bent upon him as though fascinated. He gazed back, caught in their spell, but it was not one of magic. His will was free, and he could act as he chose, do what he wished. Nor did he forget Aranloth's warning about the power they possessed and their charge to protect the tombs.

And yet they were beautiful, and in that was a spell of its own; one that was stronger, deeper and more dangerous than any magic brought forth into the world of men since time began.

Kareste slapped him. It was a heavy blow, fueled by some desperate emotion.

"The words!" she yelled at him. "The charm!"

Brand reeled from the force of her fury, and he remembered his purpose here, for beauty or not, harakgar or not, still he must leave this place with Shurilgar's staff.

He straightened and spoke: *Har nere ferork. Skigg gar see!*

Many things happened as Aranloth's charm filled the tombs. The lights in the fissure spun and whirled in a frenzy. The three figures of the harakgar stiffened. The singing ceased, but not all sound, for now they hissed at him. Their long tongues writhed in their mouths like snakes, and their hair stood on end. The lights of the fissure suddenly winked out, and shadow took the bridge.

Silence fell, dismal after the singing, reminding him that he was far beneath the earth, and he felt the great dark closing in and also the weight of earth and rock and stone, and the very river that flowed high above it all out in the sunlight, the golden sunlight that he might never see again.

"Sorry," he said, turning to Kareste.

"Lead on!" she answered.

They went forward. Whether the harakgar were still there, or the charm had banished them, Brand did not know. But on they went and they were not followed. At least, not by anything that he saw or sensed, but having felt the presence of the harakgar once, he thought he would know if they were close, and they were not, but they were not far away either. Somewhere in the uneasy tombs they waited.

Ahead of them a vast chamber opened up. The mist beneath their feet that Kareste had called swelled and flowed and gave off a greater light to fill the space.

It was a grand place. Marble flagging lined the floor, and benches of the same stone were set in rows. Here was a place where people rested, and looking up at the walls Brand saw carvings that confirmed his thought. For he saw there a great procession of men and women.

They followed an ox-drawn cart, and their heads were low and tears streamed down their cheeks. It was a funerary procession, of that he had no doubt, and the mourners on the wall sat in such a place as he stood in now while robe-clad figures at the head of the cart performed some rite. That they spoke was clear, and he realized that in their mouths was the very same charm that he had uttered himself.

He said it again, for though there was no sense of danger, he had not felt one last time either. Immediately, the light seemed brighter, and the great chamber not so old and remote as the dimmer light had made it seem.

They walked to the center. The noise of their steps was loud, echoing from the vaulted roof high above, no matter how softly they paced. Here was another crossroads.

Brand thought, reaching back to what Aranloth had told him about this place. Kareste remained silent by his side.

If she was surprised that he did not take any of the paths, but instead headed for a carving on the left wall, she did not show it.

They came to a halt before the wall. Here were many carvings in bas-relief. Brand studied them, seeing even the grooves here and there of a chisel. It was a strange thing to see. The art looked as though it was made yesterday, yet it was crafted in a time older even than legend. The Letharn were myth, and yet it seemed that even the myths of Alithoras were real. It was a sobering thought, because it made him question all that he knew and caused him to wonder what other powers existed in the land that might yet have survived, and of which he knew nothing.

But the carvings held his attention. They stood out from the wall, giving things a look of reality as though the people there might step out of the stone and talk to him.

But he soon found the particular carving Aranloth had told him of. It was a man, tall and athletic, a spear raised in his right hand, ready to throw.

Brand reached out. His hand touched the cold surface, and then he applied force. Not a great deal, but not a light amount either. He pushed the spear, as though to propel it along the path chosen by the hurler. And the spear moved.

There was no grinding sound. Nor a click or any other noise. The spear just moved, and when it did a thin split appeared in the very wall that they looked at.

The split grew, and then there was a sound of movement, of stone rolling on stone, but it was a faint thing, barely a whisper.

Ahead of them was now a door. It was not large, and they had to duck to go through, but it was wide enough for them to pass ahead with ease.

Brand went first. Kareste's misty light followed him, and then she came herself.

Almost immediately there was a set of stairs. Of what stone they were made, Brand did not know. But it was black as the darkness around them, and there was no ornamentation.

They descended slowly. The stairs went on and on, and his legs began to ache from the repeated stepping.

At length, the stairs brought them to a narrow corridor. And though it was narrow it was decorated as the stairs were not. The flagstones and walls were of white marble, milky smooth with yellowish swirls. There were no tombs, but there was gold. There was gold everywhere, inlaid on the walls and floor, even in the ceiling above.

Brand wondered if it was poisoned like the other treasures. He thought not, for otherwise people could not walk here, but he had no intention of trying to take anything. The staff was his only concern.

Without warning the gold glimmered and sparkled. Suddenly three beasts stood at the end of the corridor. They were not wolves, though they looked like wolves. Nor were they the sorcerous beasts of the elùgroths that hunted him.

Brand knew what they were. They were the harakgar, taken another form as Aranloth had warned they could. And if they were beautiful before, they were hideous now.

The beast-harakgar began to snarl. White teeth flashed. Red tongues lolled. Saliva dripped to the floor.

"How did the things hunting us get in here?" hissed Kareste.

"No," he answered. "These are not the sendings of the Elùgroths. These are the harakgar. Their form changes, but the feel of their presence does not."

He saw that she gave him a peculiar look.

"Didn't Aranloth tell you that they can take any form?" he asked.

"Yes, I suppose he did, but I still didn't see the difference as swiftly as you."

She gazed at him once more with those green-brown eyes as though he were something strange, but he had no time to think about it.

The harakgar began to pad along the bridge, and he voiced Aranloth's charm one again. *Har nere ferork. Skigg gar skee.*

182

The beasts cocked their heads and looked at him, ears pricked.

Har nere ferork. Skigg gar skee, he said again, louder.

The light in the passageway flickered. The beasts stood unmoving. Yet the stone about their feet no longer seemed solid. Instead, it rippled like water and the harakgar sank into it, their long ears the last thing to disappear.

Brand moved ahead. Kareste came with him. They passed over the spot where the beasts had stood, but there was no sign of them, nor any sense of their presence nearby.

Kareste trod warily, but he walked over the stone with confidence. Soon a new noise began. It was a dull tinkling that gradually became louder. They glanced at each other but did not speak. Neither of them knew what it was.

Eventually they came to another chamber. It was a great dome. Beaten gold plated the walls. The floors were flagged with colored mosaics. Strange symbols swirled in endless shapes and patterns beneath their boots.

From the center of the dome a column of water rushed and whispered, falling from on high in a direct line.

The water did not gather inside a basin. Rather, it gushed into a gold-rimmed hole in the ground. Before the streaming water a throne was set. Ringing it in a half circle were thirteen lesser thrones. Or perhaps they were only grand chairs, signifying some high station, but not the highest. They were tall backed and oddly shaped. Once, maybe, they had been cushioned, but if so that material had long since turned into a fine dust that lay thick on the seats. And the seats were of gold and the backs of ivory swirled with silver.

Brand looked up. High above, the ceiling was black; not the black of darkness, for Kareste's light reached there, but the black of some dark stone. It was, perhaps, jet. But it was not stone alone. Glittering from the black dome were thousands of lights that winked and shimmered. It looked like a replica of the starry sky, and so it was, for he soon saw many constellations that he knew, including bright Halathgar. But it was not stars that shone upon him, reflecting Kareste's light, but a vast treasure of jewels and gems. And a pale moon hung there also, a silver crescent worth a king's ransom.

"What *is* this place?" Kareste whispered, and the gem-stars seemed to shimmer and tremble at the sound of her voice.

"Where the ancient priests met," he answered. "So much Aranloth told me. But he said nothing of the wealth."

Kareste looked around. "There are thirteen chairs," she said. "That's a number favored by elùgroths. The Lòhrenin is a council of twelve."

She stepped closer to one of the chairs, but was careful not to touch it. He saw that they were of a strange design, both the seat and the backs being triangular in shape.

And he saw also what he had not noticed earlier: there was writing on the backs in the strange script of the Letharn.

"What does it say?" he asked.

Kareste peered for several moments, shifting her gaze from one seat to another.

"They're names, I think. I see Ubrik and Fikril. I see Dilik and Barak-bar. I see..." here she paused for a long while as she studied the thirteenth. There was an expression on her high-cheeked face that Brand could not read.

184

"Here also I see the name of Harlak," she said at last and turned to him, her eyes widened by awe. "That translates to 'noble might' from the tongue of the Letharn, even as Aranloth has the same meaning in the speech of the Halathrin."

She said no more. And though Brand now understood the strange emotion that ran through her, he saw something else.

On another seat, even as the lòhren told him it would be, he saw the object of his quest. It rested on the third chair from the left, wrapped in tattered cloth, but the dark end of a shattered staff stuck out. He knew what it was.

Kareste looked also, and she studied the writing on that chair also.

"Here the name translates as 'midnight star,' which is what Shurilgar means."

Brand reached out slowly. The cloth fell to dust at his touch, and beneath lay a black wych-wood staff. Well he knew it, for he had seen the other half.

He picked it up, feeling a strange thrill at its touch that was more than excitement.

But he had no time to reflect on what he sensed, for many things now happened at once.

He felt suddenly dizzy as though he were in two places at once, and a force of malice struck him as a blow. The thing was not as Aranloth's staff, an artifact imbued with power: this talisman took it to a far higher level. Magic swirled and flowed and oozed from it with raw power. A great black stream shot up his arm, into his body, and up to his head. Aranloth's diadem flared, and as swift as he had felt dizzy, now he was clear headed again.

A moment he had to choose, to accept the power and let it flow into him, to join with him. Or to reject it utterly.

And one other thing he knew. The black staff was broken, yet he felt its other half now with great clarity. It throbbed and pulsed far away to the north. He sensed even the elùgroths that touched it, that worked some great sorcery. And they sensed him. Their power was immense, and unified, yet something else lay behind it. Some force, far, far more remote, far greater than they, yet it sustained them. Away over countless leagues and beyond many plains and rivers and mountains a mind stirred: vast, imponderable, drenched in ancient enmity. It guided and uplifted the others.

Brand withdrew. He pulled his mind away from the staff, from all that it showed him. Black fire flared, then subsided. The staff was cold in his hand and dark again. The senses he had were lost.

He turned, and saw that Kareste was looking at him as though he were the strangest thing in the tombs. It was not for the first time. He was about to speak, but then he saw what was behind her.

"The harakgar!" he yelled.

She spun to look. Lòhrengai trailed from her fingers even as she moved. But she halted in shock, seeing what he saw.

In the column of water were the three figures. Like serpents they seemed, writhing and twisting among each other as the water poured over them. But they had faces, the same high-cheeked and beautiful faces that he had seen before.

The harakgar hissed, the noise blending with the sound of the water, and then the creatures slid out of the column. Their entwined coils looped over the flagging, wetting it as they undulated.

With a final sharp hiss they separated. Suddenly, the three of them reared, now part serpent and part woman. In their hands they held high the serrated knives, and they attacked.

22. Out of Dim Legend

There was no time for thought. Brand leaped to meet them, stepping between the creatures and Kareste who seemed transfixed. He held both staffs upraised in defense. And then he yelled the charm.

The serpents hissed. They slid and coiled and arched before him, tongues angrily flicking the air.

He chanted louder, and from behind him the girl also spoke. Having heard and learned the words, she added her voice to his.

What Aranloth would say to that, Brand did not know, yet the serpents reluctantly slid back into the column of water. There they twined among themselves as they rode and swam the current, plummeting out of sight.

He ceased chanting. So did Kareste. Yet they both knew the charm was losing its force, or else having touched some item bestowed in the tombs, the power of the harakgar was increased.

Kareste faced him. "Twice now you have saved me. That puts me in your debt, for once only have I saved you."

"We need not speak of debt, you and I," Brand answered. "They say that adversity bonds people together. But adversity or no, I like you anyway. But if you would repay me, one thing alone I ask."

"What's that?"

"Tell me the truth. Now, once and for all. And swiftly. There's more going on you said when we first met than a battle for Cardoroth. I gave those words less

188

heed than I should have, for just now I felt … something when I picked up the broken staff. And a name, maybe, I could put to it. One out of dim legend."

She eyed him without speaking, but at length she sighed.

"Very well. I'll tell you what I know, and more maybe of what I guess. We have little time. The harakgar will allow us small respite, yet while we rest, without trying to take the staff away, they will endure our presence the better, I think. And rest we must, for when we go they'll not hold back their power. Rather, I think it will increase the closer we get to the outside world."

They sat down on the mosaicked flagging before the ancient chairs. Strange they would have looked, in that ancient and domed room, where once great councils and ceremonies were held. But to them, in their tiredness, a seat was a seat and they dared not sit on the chairs.

"I know what it was that you felt in the staff," Kareste said. "Or rather through it. Others, though deeper steeped in lore and power, have felt the same thing. You should not feel it. But the broken staff, and Aranloth's staff, and the diadem open your mind to these forces. Still, you sense more than you should. And with each passing day the more do I think that Aranloth chose you well. Though you're a warrior, the staff of a lòhren is not so ill-suited to you as I thought at first."

He grew agitated, and she held up a hand. "Now, I'll answer you. Yes, there's more going on. The history of these lands is enough to tell you that ever we are at war with the south; the elugs, the Azan and other creatures besides that dwell there. They have attacked and harried the north since before the founding of Cardoroth and the other Camar cities. They are our enemies, for they would overrun this land. But cast your mind back to a

189

time of legend before even ancient history. Of that, what can you say?"

"Little," he answered. "Only what every child learns in stories. That the exodus of the Halathrin brought them to our lands in pursuit of a great evil. And greater evil followed. A Shadowed Lord rose – master of the elùgroths. And war raged over the lands. Yet that great lord was thrown down at the last, though his designs and plans and minions live after him in the elùgroths."

"Thus the legends tell us," she said. "And they speak truly…"

"And yet?"

"And yet for long ages the lòhrens and the Halathrin dreaded that while this power was defeated, it was not wholly destroyed. One day, they feared, he would rise again, and gathering darkness about him start once more to complete what he had not finished in ages past."

"*Elùdrath*," he whispered. The shadows of the cavern flitted, and he felt that even the dead in the tombs all around listened to his hoarse voice.

"Yes. And you have sensed him now as others have before you, though they be greater in power."

"Very well, then," he said briskly. "All the more reason to destroy this thing. Maybe so shall Cardoroth survive, though clearly other battles will come."

He made to stand, but she raised her hand again.

"Wait," she said. "There's one thing more."

"What?"

"This only. Before the elùgroths came to Cardoroth with war, they escaped from Halathar, the forest realm of the Halathrin. Much evil they did there, but the greatest was this – somewhere in the hills of Lòrenta they loosed a great sorcery. Contrived of the half of Shurilgar's staff that they possess, they created beasts as you have seen at Lake Alithorin. But even as those hounds were made of men, these others were bound to Alithoras by Halathrin forms. Immortals of great power. They roam now in the hills, twisted by sorcery, driven by the evil that possesses them to prowl and kill and slay. And lòhrengai avails little against them, for the blood of the immortals is stronger, more enduring, surer than that of men or elug. This is an evil in itself that cannot be borne, and yet also it threatens the lòhrens. And therefore all Alithoras."

Brand brooded on the news that she gave and wondered why she had not mentioned it before. He did not like it. The dark sorcery sickened him, yet he saw no way to help, no matter how much he wanted to.

"What can I do about that?" he asked. His answer was curter than he meant, for being powerless annoyed him.

"You? You can do nothing. But me … that is a different question. I have the skill to undo the sorcery and free the immortals thus caught from torment. So I think, at least."

"Then you should not be helping me. Help them instead."

"Ahh…" she sighed. "There it is. In helping you, I *am* helping them. For ultimately, there is only one way to undo the sorcery. Perhaps I alone of all the lòhrens could achieve it. But I cannot do it with lòhrengai. The dark spell can only be undone with the same power that brought it into being. To free them, I need Shurilgar's staff."

She looked away. There was a long silence, profound within the tombs. Only the streaming column of water made any noise.

Brand stood, and she looked up at him from where she sat. There was much that he could read in her face, and much that was still hidden.

"We'll speak of this later," he said.

191

"Will you give me the staff?" she insisted.

"Truly, I don't know. For to do so would betray Aranloth's hope in me, and the king's. And perhaps allow an entire people to be murdered. Yet would they not want this other sorcery, this abomination, undone? I cannot say. And I won't decide here in the dark. When I feel the light on my face and breathe fresh air once more, and when the listening ears of the long-dead are not about me, then will I speak of it again."

"So be it," Kareste said.

Without another word they left the great chamber. But even as they took the first steps he felt the growing pressure of the harakgar on his mind. He realized that now they were roused. The charm had worked before, but whether it would hold off their waxing fury he did not know.

He spoke the words that Aranloth had given him at nearly every step, but still the pressure grew until the dead air of the tombs seemed to spark with malicious life.

They made it back to the bridge before the harakgar attacked, despite his constant voicing of the charm. But this time they dropped from the air above.

Brand spun and thrust Aranloth's staff at the nearest one. She flew on black wings, graceful as a swan, and her long hair trailed behind her in the wind of her descent.

Silver flame burst from the staff, and the shock of the impact drove him to his knees. The harakgar twisted to the side, for a moment looking less graceful, and then she rose above the bridge again.

Next to him a spray of lòhren-fire struck the other two. They screeched and hissed, fluttering higher to join their companion.

Brand and Kareste began to move across the bridge. They made it to the other side, and though Brand repeated the charm, this time the harakgar did not go away. They hovered in the high shadows, and the deep lights in the chasm far below spun wildly.

The two of them ran. As best they could they watched behind them. The harakgar followed, gliding down and then running swiftly on long legs, their wings gone but their shadowy hair still trailing behind them.

The clamor of the chase was loud. Surely no such noise had been heard here in the dark amid the dead in all the endless years of their rest. Brand had a sudden and stabbing fear – the dead would begin to wake. He tried to put the thought from his mind, but the pounding of his boots seemed to drive the fear through his body, and the echo of the chase ran ahead of them all, stirring other strange noises to life.

Behind, the harakgar screeched and leaped. He lifted Aranloth's staff, fighting off all three. No fire burst from it this time. The creatures bashed it from his grip before he was ready. The weight of them knocked him down, and even as his head struck the ground he heard the clatter of the falling staff somewhere away to his right.

He tried to raise Shurilgar's broken staff, but the harakgar were upon him. They weighed on him like stone statues come to life, and the strength of them was beyond any man. They pinned him, their hot breath beat upon him like wild beasts, and their long hair billowed and rolled in choking masses over his face.

But half blinded as he was, he saw the serrated knives rise as one. He made a last effort to throw the creatures off, but one hand caught him by the throat and squeezed like the death-grip that it was.

Then suddenly he was blinded by light. A great roar filled his ears. The harakgar screeched. He saw lòhrengai take their arms, melting flesh from bone.

The screams filled his ears and suddenly the weight was off him. He gasped for breath, struggled to grab Aranloth's staff and used it to prop himself up.

Kareste stood between him and the three harakgar. She screamed in her own turn, but it was in fury rather than pain. Back the harakgar ran, disappearing into the tunnel behind them, swallowed by the dark.

The two of them looked at each other. He felt the slow drip of blood along his arms, but he did not think he was badly hurt. His neck ached, and he realized that even without the knives the harakgar were close to killing him. A moment longer and they would have broken his neck.

Kareste had fared better, yet she had used so much of her power that she now seemed exhausted. They moved ahead, neither having the strength to run or even speak.

On they went, near-dead things themselves, ignoring the alcoves and the bodies and the treasures that lay to either side. Fresh air and light were the treasures they sought.

And ahead, tantalizingly close, was the dim outline of the cave entrance. But something shuffled toward them, silhouetted by the pale light of the outside world.

Brand and Kareste went forward to meet this new challenge, but their strength had not recovered. They needed rest, but that they would not have unless they broke out of the tombs.

The figures ahead drew near. There were three, but they were not the harakgar; at least, if they were, they had taken yet another form. For what approached now were warriors. Tall they stood, proud and stern. White tunics gleamed and their silver-helmed faces shone with a pale light. Golden hair spilled over their shoulders. Their eyes were keen, and in their hands they held bright swords.

He recognized the design of both helm and sword. He wore something similar on his own head, and carried something alike at his side.

On came the warriors, now stalking toward them with a grace that no man could match.

"Halathrin!" Kareste whispered fiercely.

"Yes and no," he replied. "Remember the skeletons we saw as we came in? These are they – Halathrin, but long dead. The harakgar have raised them, put upon them the guise they wore in life."

Kareste looked at him, and he saw the fear in her eyes. But he had no words. That same fear was in his own, and she saw it.

Close as they were to escape, this last battle seemed too much. How could they kill the already dead?

There was no more time to think. The lead warrior drove at him with a gleaming blade. Brand stepped aside, deflecting it with Aranloth's staff, but the warrior was quicker than any he had fought before. Straightaway the white-clad attacker turned and thrust his blade again.

Brand retreated. Beside him, Kareste did likewise. Fire lashed out from her fingers. It lit the tunnel with a sizzle of light and heat, but when it subsided the warriors were still there, advancing upon them, driving them deeper into the tombs.

"The staff!" Kareste called. "Give me Shurilgar's staff!"

He stepped back another pace, caught in fear and uncertainty. Dare he give it to her? Did he trust her? Would it be destroyed, or would Cardoroth fall instead?"

"The staff!" she screamed again.

Brand hardened his resolve. Cardoroth must not fall. He stopped his backward movement. The Halathrin looked at him, eyes as keen as swords, but their real blades flickered with a pale light as though a fire burned within them.

He took a firm grip on Aranloth's staff. Thrice he struck it down upon the stone. The Halathrin did not move. The tombs waited until the slow echoes died away. And then Brand shouted in a clear voice.

Har nere ferork. Skigg gar skee!

And as he voiced the charm he summoned the last of his strength. He thought nothing of the blades and battle and the warfare that he knew. He drew on some deeper part of his mind that was waking, though he did not want to admit it, and from his inner self a fire sprang. It leaped from him into Aranloth's staff, and there it burned, hot as the sun, before it rushed out in a stream from its tip.

The Halathrin that were harakgar staggered back. Their long hair burned. Their green eyes caught fire and sizzled. They reeled away, and as they did he reached out, seeking for the remnant of whatever had once been their own, for that part of them that was not the harakgar.

He glimpsed a brief vision of faraway lands. There were trees and light and singing and beauty. As though some door suddenly opened, what was left of the Halathrin fled away. Their form fell from the harakgar, and there the three sisters stood again, naked, pressed back against the wall, but already he saw their hair begin to grow back, and the light come once more into their eyes.

"Run!" he yelled.

Kareste was with him. They sped up the last part of the tunnel. Darkness rolled behind them, gathering pace like a storm about to break, and then they were out of the cave, sprawling to the ground into the light and beyond the reach of their attackers.

A dark wind shrieked behind them, whistling at the entrance of the cave, but it swiftly faltered.

"We have it!" Brand said. 'The quest is ours!"

He staggered to his feet, looking for Kareste, feeling the glory of the sun. He saw instead something that stole the joy from his heart and flooded his mind with despair.

The horses remained where they had been left, but beyond stood Khamdar. He towered above Brand, who was a big man himself, and the elùgroth looked down upon him with cold eyes. There was also a band of elugs, scimitars drawn and three hounds, tongues dripping sweat, and a low growl in their throats.

Brand sensed Kareste moving close to him. She was spent, as was he, and their enemies ringed them. The only place to retreat was into the tombs, and he hoped never to go in there again. Better to face death in the sun than in the dark.

Khamdar spoke, and his voice was quiet, yet full of confidence.

"Long was the chase, but the hunt is over. Now you shall learn what it means to defy an elùgroth. It is a lesson few need teaching, and of those who do, none live to beg for mercy."

Brand did not answer. He still struggled to breathe. But next to him, Kareste spoke softly.

"Give it to me," she said.

Brand knew what she meant. He did not know what powers she could draw from Shurilgar's staff, but he knew that it would aid her.

"Give it to me!" she said more fiercely. "It's our only hope."

Brand hesitated. While he stood there in doubt, the elùgroth flicked his cold gaze between them.

"Wise are you to mistrust," he said. "For she commands great power – even without the staff. But with it – with it, she could be a great one. Great among elùgroths." He turned to her, his dark eyes black pits. "Is it not so? I sense the power of elùgai in you. Though blended with the taint of lòhrengai."

He turned back to Brand with a fierce smile. "Yes. Give her the staff. It will be the final step in her transformation. And well would she wield it."

Brand swayed and the world spun around him. He felt the truth in what the elùgroth said. Yet was it the whole truth?

Thus ends *Raging Swords*. The Durlindrath series will continue soon in book two, *Defiant Swords*, where Brand learns more of the threat to Alithoras and faces his greatest challenge yet.

Sign up below and be the first to hear about new book releases, see previews and learn of upcoming discounts. http://eepurl.com/Rswv1

Visit my website at www.homeofhighfantasy.com

Encyclopedic Glossary

Many races dwell in Alithoras. All have their own language, and though sometimes related to one another, the changes sparked by migration, isolation and various influences often render these tongues unintelligible to each other.

The ascendancy of Halathrin culture, combined with their widespread efforts to secure and maintain allies against elug incursions, has made their language the primary means of communication between diverse peoples.

For instance, a soldier of Cardoroth addressing a ship's captain from Camarelon would speak Halathrin, or a simplified version of it, even though their native speeches stem from the same ancestral language.

This glossary contains a range of names and terms. Many are of Halathrin origin, and their meaning is provided. The remainder derive from native tongues and are obscure, so meanings are only given intermittently.

Some variation exists within the Halathrin language, chiefly between the regions of Halathar and Alonin. The most obvious example is the latter's preference for a "dh" spelling instead of "th".

Often, Camar names and Halathrin elements are combined. This is especially so for the aristocracy. No other tribes had such long-term friendship with the Halathrin, and though in this relationship they lost some of their natural culture, they gained nobility and knowledge in return.

List of abbreviations:

Azn. Azan

Cam. Camar

Chg. Cheng

Comb. Combined

Cor. Corrupted form

Duth. Duthenor

Esg. Esgallien

Hal. Halathrin

Leth. Letharn

Prn. Pronounced

Alithoras: *Hal.* "Silver land." The Halathrin name for the continent they settled after the exodus. Refers to the extensive river and lake systems they found and their appreciation of the beauty of the land.

Alith Nien: *Hal.* "Silver river." Has its source in the mountainous lands of Auren Dennath and empties into Lake Alithorin.

Anast Dennath: *Hal.* "Stone mountains." Mountain range in northern Alithoras. Contiguous with Auren Dennath and location of the Dweorhrealm.

Angle: The land hemmed in by the Carist Nien and Erenian rivers, especially the area in proximity to their divergence.

Arach Neben: *Hal.* "West gate." The great wall surrounding Cardoroth has four gates. Each is named after a cardinal direction, and each also carries a token to represent a celestial object. Arach Neben bears a steel ornament of the Morning Star.

Aranloth: *Hal.* "Noble might." A lòhren.

Aurellin: *Cor. Hal.* The first element means blue. The second appears to be native Camar. Queen of Cardoroth and wife to Gilhain.

Auren Dennath: *Comb. Duth.* and *Hal. Prn.* Our-ren dennath. "Blue mountains." Mountain range in northern Alithoras. Contiguous with Anast Dennath.

Azan: *Azn.* Desert dwelling people. Their nobility often serve as leaders of elug armies. They are a prideful race, often haughty and domineering, but they also adhere to a strict code of honor.

Barak-bar: *Leth.* A long-dead priest who served in ancient times within the tombs of the Letharn.

Brand: A Duthenor tribesman. Currently serving King Gilhain as his Durlindrath.

Camar: *Cam. Prn.* Kay-mar. A race of interrelated tribes that migrated in two main stages. The first brought them to the vicinity of Halathar; in the second, they separated and established cities along a broad sweep of eastern Alithoras.

Camarelon: *Cam. Prn.* Kam-arelon. A port city and capital of a Camar tribe. It was founded before Cardoroth as the waves of migrating people settled the more southerly lands first. Each new migration tended northward. It is perhaps the most representative of a traditional Camar realm.

Carangar: *Hal.* "Car - red, angar - outcrop of rock or something prominent that juts from the surface of the land or another object." A Durlin.

Cardoroth: *Cor. Hal. Comb. Cam.* A Camar city, often called Red Cardoroth. Some say this alludes to the red granite commonly used in the construction of its buildings, others that it refers to a prophecy of destruction.

Cardurleth: *Hal.* "Car - red, dur - steadfast, leth - stone." The great wall that surrounds Cardoroth. Established soon after the city's founding and constructed with red granite. It looks displeasing to the eye, but the people of the city love it nonetheless. They believe it impregnable and say that no enemy shall ever breach it – except by treachery.

Careth Nien: *Hal. Prn.* Kareth nyen. "Great river." Largest river in Alithoras. Has its source in the mountains of Anast Dennath and runs southeast across the land before emptying into the sea. It was over this river (which sometimes freezes along its northern stretches) that the Camar and other tribes migrated into the eastern lands. Much later, Brand came to the city of Cardoroth by one of these ancient migratory routes.

Carist Nien: *Hal.* "Ice river." A river of northern Alithoras that has its source in the hills of Lòrenta.

Carnhaina: First element native *Cam.* Second *Hal.* "Heroine." An ancient queen of Cardoroth. Revered as a saviour of her people, but to some degree also feared, for she possessed powers of magic. Hated to this day by elùgroths, because she overthrew their power unexpectedly at a time when their dark influence was rising.

Carnyx horn: The sacred horn of the Camar tribes. An instrument of brass, man high with a mouth fashioned in the likeness of a fierce animal, often a boar or bear. Winded in battle and designed to intimidate the foe with its otherworldly sound. Some believe it invokes supernatural aid.

Chapterhouse: Special halls set aside in the palace of Cardoroth for the private meetings, teachings and military training of the Durlin.

Crenel: The vertical gap on a battlement between merlons. The merlon offers protection, the crenel an opening through which missiles are fired.

Dilik: A long-dead priest who served in ancient times within the tombs of the Letharn.

Drùghoth: *Hal.* First element - black. Second element - that which hastens, races or glides. More commonly called a sending.

Durlin: *Hal.* "The steadfast." The original Durlin were the seven sons of the first king of Cardoroth. They guarded him against all enemies, of which there were many, and three died to protect him. Their tradition continued throughout Cardoroth's history, suspended only once, and briefly, some four hundred years ago when it was discovered that three members were secretly in the service of elùgroths. These were imprisoned, but committed suicide while waiting for the king's trial to commence. It is rumored that the king himself provided them with the knives that they used. It is said that he felt sorry for them and gave them this way out to avoid the shame a trial would bring to their families.

Durlin creed: These are the native Camar words, long remembered and much honored, uttered by the first Durlin to die while he defended his father, and king, from attack. Tum del conar – El dar tum! Death or infamy – I choose death!

Durlindrath: *Hal.* "Lord of the steadfast." The title given to the leader of the Durlin.

Duthenor: *Duth. Prn.* Dooth-en-or. "The people." A single tribe, or sometimes a group of tribes melded into a larger people at times of war or disaster, who generally live a rustic and peaceful lifestyle. They are raisers of cattle and herders of sheep. However, when need demands they are fierce warriors – men and women alike.

Elugs: *Hal.* "That which creeps in shadows." A cruel and superstitious race that inhabits the southern lands, especially the Graèglin Dennath.

Elùdrath: *Hal. Prn.* Eloo-drath. "Shadowed lord." A sorcerer. First and greatest among elùgroths. Believed to be dead or defeated.

Elùgai: *Hal. Prn.* Eloo-guy. "Shadowed force." The sorcery of an elùgroth.

Elùgroth: *Hal. Prn.* Eloo-groth. "Shadowed horror." A sorcerer. They often take names in the Halathrin tongue in mockery of the lòhren's practice to do so.

Elu-haraken: *Hal.* "The shadowed wars." Long ago battles in a time that is become myth to the Camar tribes.

Erenian River: A river in northern Alithoras. Some say its name derives from a corruption of the Halathrin word "nien," meaning river. Others dispute this and postulate the word derives from a pre-exodus name adopted by the Camar tribes after they settled the east of Alithoras.

Exodus: The arrival of the Halathrin into Alithoras from an outside land. They came by ship and beached north of Anast Dennath.

Faladir: A city founded by a Camar tribe.

Fikril: A long-dead priest who served in ancient times within the tombs of the Letharn.

Foresight: Premonition of the future. Can occur at random as a single image or as a longer sequence of events. Can also be deliberately sought by entering the realm between life and death where the spirit is released from the body to travel through space and time. To achieve this, the body must be brought to the very threshold of death. The first method is uncontrollable and rare. The second exceedingly rare but controllable for those with the skill and willingness to endure the danger.

Free Cities: A group of cooperative city states that pool military resources to defend themselves against attack. Founded prior to Cardoroth. Initially ruled by kings and queens, now by a senate.

Galenthern: *Hal.* "Green flat." Southern plains bounded by the Careth Nien and the Graèglin Dennath mountain range.

Gernlik: *Cam.* A Durlin.

Gilhain: *Comb. Cam & Hal.* First element unknown, second "hero." King of Cardoroth. Husband to Aurellin.

Graèglin Dennath: *Hal. Prn.* Greg-lin dennath. "Mountains of ash." Chain of mountains in southern Alithoras. The landscape is one of jagged stone and boulder, relieved only by gaping fissures from which plumes of ashen smoke ascend, thus leading to its name. Believed to be impassable because of the danger of poisonous air flowing from cracks, and the ground unexpectedly giving way, swallowing any who dare to tread its forbidden paths. In other places swathes of molten stone run in rivers down its slopes.

Great North Road: An ancient construction of the Halathrin. Built at a time when they had settlements in the northern reaches of Alithoras. Warriors traveled swiftly from north to south in order to aid the main population who dwelt in Halathar when they faced attack from the south.

Grothanon: *Hal.* "Horror desert." The flat salt plains south of the Graèglin Dennath.

Halathar: *Hal.* "Dwelling place of the people of Halath." The forest realm of the Halathrin.

Halathgar: *Hal.* "Bright star." Actually a constellation. Also known as the Lost Huntress.

Halathrin: *Hal.* "People of Halath." A race named after a mighty lord who led an exodus of his people to the continent of Alithoras in pursuit of justice, having sworn to redress a great evil. They are human, though of fairer form, greater skill and higher culture. They possess an inherent unity of body, mind and spirit enabling insight and endurance beyond other races of Alithoras. Reported to be immortal, but killed in great numbers during their conflicts with the evil they seek to destroy. Those conflicts are collectively known as the elù-haraken: the Shadowed Wars.

Harakgar: *Leth.* The three sisters. Creatures of magic brought into being by the lore of the Letharn. Their purpose is to protect the tombs of their creators from robbery.

Harlak: *Leth.* An ancient name of Aranloth.

Harath Neben: *Hal.* "North gate." This gate bears a token of two massive emeralds that represent the constellation of Halathgar. The gate is also known as "Hunter's Gate," for the north road out of the city leads to wild lands full of game.

Immortals: See Halathrin.

Kareste: A mysterious girl who helps Brand. She possess potent magic.

Khamdar: An elùgroth. Leader of the host the besieges Cardoroth.

Lake Alithorin: *Hal.* "Silver lake." A lake of northern Alithoras.

Letharn: *Hal.* "Stone raisers. Builders." A race of people that in antiquity ruled much of Alithoras. Only traces of their civilization remain.

Lethrin: *Hal.* "Stone people." Creatures of the Graèglin Dennath. Renowned for their size and strength. Tunnelers and miners.

Lòhren: *Hal. Prn.* Ler-ren. "Knowledge giver – a counsellor." Other terms used by various nations include wizard, druid and sage.

Lòhren-fire: A defensive manifestation of lòhrengai. The color of the flame varies according to the skill and temperament of the lòhren.

Lòhrengai: *Hal. Prn.* Ler-ren-guy. "Lòhren force." Enchantment, spell or use of arcane power. A manipulation and transformation of the natural energy

209

inherent in all things. Each use takes something from the user. Likewise, some part of the transformed energy infuses them. Lòhrens use it sparingly, elùgroths indiscriminately.

Lòhrenin: *Hal. Prn.* Ler-ren-in. "Council of lòhrens."

Lòrenta: *Hal. Prn.* Ler-rent-a. "Hills of knowledge." Uplands in northern Alithoras in which the stronghold of the lòhrens is established.

Lornach: A Durlin. Friend to Brand and often called by his nickname of "Shorty."

Lost Huntress: See Halathgar.

Magic: Supernatural power. See lòhrengai and elùgai.

Menetuin: A city on the east coast of Alithoras. Founded by the Camar.

Merlon: The vertical stonework on a battlement between crenels. The merlon offers protection, the crenel a gap through which missiles are fired.

Otherworld: Camar term for a mingling of half-remembered history, myth and the spirit world.

Sellic Neben: *Hal.* "East gate." This gate bears a representation, crafted of silver and pearl, of the moon rising over the sea.

Sending: See Drùghoth.

Shadowed Lord: See Elùdrath.

Shazrahad: The Azan who commands an elug army, or serves as a lieutenant of an elùgroth.

Shuffa: A type of boat. Small, fast and ideal for travel by river. Favored by the villagers who dwell along the Careth Nien, and based on a design originating from ancient times when the Letharn fished the two rivers of the Angle. The same name is used in Cardoroth for a different kind of boat, slower and of a different shape. It's unclear which version is closer to the original design.

Shurilgar: *Hal.* "Midnight star." An elùgroth. Also called the betrayer of nations.

Sorcerer: See Elùgroth.

Sorcery: See elùgai.

Surcoat: An outer garment. Often worn over chain mail. The Durlin surcoat is unadorned white.

Taingern: *Cam.* A Durlin. Friend to Brand.

Tombs of the Letharn: The ancient burial place of the Letharn people. All members of the population, throughout the course of their long civilization, were laid to rest here. It was believed that to be interred elsewhere was to condemn the spirit to a true death, rather than an afterlife. The dead were preserved, and returned even from the far reaches of the empire. This was withheld from perpetrators of treason and heinous crimes. These were buried in special cemeteries near the river. Petty criminals were afforded an opportunity to redeem their place in the tombs on payment of a fine determined by the head-priest.

Ubrik: A long-dead priest who served in ancient times within the tombs of the Letharn.

Unlach Neben: *Hal.* "South gate." This gate bears a representation of the sun, crafted of gold, beating down upon a desert land. Said by some to signify the homeland of the elugs, whence the gold of the sun was obtained by an adventurer of old.

War drums: Drums of the elug tribes. Used especially in times of war or ceremony. Rumored to carry hidden messages in their beat and also to invoke sorcery.

Wizard: See lòhren.

Wych-wood: A general description for a range of supple and springy timbers. Some hardy varieties are prevalent on the poisonous slopes of the Graèglin Dennath mountain range and are favored by elùgroths as instruments of sorcery.

From the author

I'm a man born in the wrong era. My heart yearns for faraway places and even further afield times. Tolkien had me at the beginning of *The Hobbit* when he said, ". . . one morning long ago in the quiet of the world . . ."

Sometimes I imagine myself in a Viking mead-hall. The long winter night presses in, but the shimmering embers of a log in the hearth hold back both cold and dark. The chieftain calls for a story, and I take a sip from my drinking horn and stand up . . .

Or maybe the desert stars shine bright and clear, obscured occasionally by wisps of smoke from burning camel dung. A dry gust of wind marches sand grains across our lonely campsite, and the wayfarers about me stir restlessly. I sip cool water and begin to speak.

I'm a storyteller. A man to paint a picture by the slow music of words. I like to bring faraway places and times to life, to make hearts yearn for something they can never have, unless for a passing moment.